A
PARANORMAL CASEBOOK

Robert Lee Dean

Edited by
J. N. McLaughlin & R.L. Dean

Illustrated by
Crissha Figarella

This book is dedicated to all the Law Enforcement
Officers who, in the course of their career, have
stumbled on to cases and situations that defy
normal explanation ...

CONTENTS

FOREWORD

Here in contains, 21 stories from the casebook of Robert Lee Dean, a cop on patrol across the long, and lonely highways of West Texas ...

One of greatest challenges of editing is maintaining the author's style and character. The temptation is always there to correct every sentence, put periods and commas in, dividing the structure into a strict language as designed by a bunch of college English professors. This can turn an entertaining story into a technical manual. With that in mind, James and I as editors, have done our best to keep dad's original creative use of language to express tense, voice, and mood. On occasion, we have corrected spelling or placed a comma here and there for clarification. Some cleanup in format was necessary due in large part to the medium in which his original stories were distributed.

The task of creating a *casebook* was made possible by Doug Klein, who collected dad's Facebook posts over the years and put them together. He also came up with a darn good blurb. Without his help this project would have been short lived. Thanks Doug.

—Ron

As with all books published under RLD Publications, LLC, regardless of genre, a clear gospel message will be presented in the foreword. I encourage you to read it:

The Gospel Call

"In accordance with the Father's good pleasure, the eternal Son, who is equal with the Father and is the exact representation of His nature, willingly left the glory of heaven, was conceived by the Holy Spirit in the womb of a virgin, and was born the God-man: Jesus of Nazareth. As a man, He walked on this earth in perfect obedience to the law of God. In the fullness of time, men rejected and crucified Him. On the cross, He bore man's sin, suffered God's wrath, and died in man's place. On the third day, God raised Him from the dead. This resurrection is the divine declaration that the Father has accepted His Son's death as a sacrifice for sin. Jesus paid the penalty for man's disobedience, satisfied the demands of justice, and appeased the wrath of God. Forty days after the resurrection, the Son of God ascended into the heavens, sat down at the right hand of the Father, and was given glory, honor, and dominion over all. There, in the presence of God, He represents His people and makes requests to God on their behalf. All who acknowledge their sinful, helpless state and throw themselves upon Christ, God will fully pardon, declare righteous, and reconcile unto Himself. This is the gospel of God and of Jesus Christ, His Son."

—*Taken from the Gospel Call*, Paul Washer

If you have any questions about the scriptures or Jesus, please contact me at http://www.genericscifi.com.

A ROSE FOR ROSE

West Texas. Miles and miles of ... miles and miles. Two lane blacktop and dirt roads into desolate places. I was a deputy at a rural Sheriff's Department. Working night shift on a hot summer night when I happened upon her grave, on a long lonely stretch of dirt road to a ranch somewhere. My car headlights happen to catch the small headstone as I turned a corner. Just off the road. By itself. I stopped. Curious Cop that I am. I grabbed my flashlight and walked over to see the small weathered headstone ... tilted to one side. The barely visible name on the stone said: Rose Elizabeth Carter 1903–1911.

A little girl. Eight years old.

As I looked down on her grave I wondered. What happened? How did you end up out here ... alone? I stood there awhile. Then turned to leave, and as I did, I thought I heard faint ... crying. I stopped and listened. *Nah*. Nothing now. My imagination. The next day, silly old Cop that I am, I went to the local flower shop and bought a single rose. For

Rose. That night I returned to her grave. Just me and her, out there. I walked over and leaned down and placed the rose on her grave. I stayed a few minutes. Not knowing why I had done that. I turned to leave. Walked toward my Patrol Car and a slight breeze came up. And a small voice, distinctly said, "Thank you."

I stopped. Listened. Nothing.

My damn imagination again. I turned and looked at her grave, and the breeze had blown the single rose against her headstone. I got a chill. And said, "Your welcome. Rest now. Rest."

The old patrol car groaned to life as the sun came up on the West Texas horizon. The dust kicked up behind the car as I drove away. A new day. I needed sleep. My sleep ... for a while. Her's eternal ... A rose for Rose. The least I could do ...

PROWLER

And so, it came to pass that I had been dispatched to a "prowler" call in a neighborhood out in a rural area. At the risk of sounding like an old horror movie it was in fact ... a dark and stormy night. Rain, lightning, thunder. About 2 AM. I was the only car on that lonely stretch of two lane. The windshield wipers on my old patrol car trying to keep up with the rain. As I drove, I realized I was coming up on the location of a car accident I had been dispatched to a week before. Raining that night, too. I was the first on the scene that night. The other units and the ambulance not yet arriving. I turned on my "overheads" and pulled over at the sight of an overturned vehicle. I exited my patrol car to a see a young girl lying in the rain swollen ditch. I ran to her and leaned over her to see her head was at an odd angle. I felt no pulse. She was gone. She was maybe 12 or 13, I figured. Blue jeans, sweatshirt, no shoes. Soaking wet from the rain pouring down. Very pretty little girl. But nothing I or anyone could do for her. The ambulance and other units arrived, and the girl's parents, it was later discovered, were found in the front seat. Still alive. They were loaded in the ambulance. The little girl had been thrown from the car when it had overturned. Broke her neck on impact.

As I drove toward that horrible scene from the week before ... I saw her. The little girl. In the headlights of my car. Standing on the side of the road. Her wet hair and clothes. Barefoot.

It was her. No doubt.

I glanced at her as I drove past. Could see her face. Sad. I didn't slow down as I drove past. No use. I had long since stopped trying to rationalize the things I had seen as a cop. I was in route to a call and had to go there. Cops have a saying— "If my mind could forget what my eyes have seen ..."

I drove on through the rain.

SHADOW WALKER

The call had been dispatched as "lights flickering" in a building. 3 AM. Okay. There be a lot of reasons for that. Power fluctuation, a short, etc. While in route, Dispatch advised that the "key holder/owner" had been notified and was on the way.

Took me about ten minutes to get there. It was a standalone building next to other older shops. No street lights. Dark. I pulled up, parking just down from the front door. You don't park in front of a suspicious call like that. Just SOP. I opened my car door and got out. Flashlight in hand, I eased down the sidewalk to the front of the building. Dark. But, sure enough ... a light "flickered" toward the back of the building. An old peeling "hardware" sign painted on the store front. A glance at the large plate glass fronting the sidewalk was intact. No signs of any breakage. I walked to the front door. Gave it a "shake". Locked tight. No signs of forced entry. I then walked down the side of the building to the back. No windows along the side of the building. I turned the corner and walked to the rear door. Locked tight. No signs of forced entry. No broken windows. Nothing. I walked back around to the front and stood waiting for the owner to arrive. Watching the little flickering of the light in back. Yeah. A power surge, a short ... whatever. I waited.

Maybe five minutes and a car pulled up. Guy gets out. Blue jeans, wrinkled shirt and house shoes. Yeah. Got woke up from a sound sleep. Younger guy. He walked up ... muttering to himself. He looked at me and said, "What, now?"

Well, *now* I explained was the flickering light in the back.

"One damned thing after another with this place," he grumbled.

He then related he had bought the building a couple of weeks ago with the intention of renovating it and making it an "art gallery." But it had one been delay after another. Workers refusing to work alone saying that weird "stuff" was happening and they were "hearing things", on and on. Tools of the workers would be found on the opposite end of the building from where they were left the day before. Lots of things happening.

I listened for a while and finally interrupted him saying I needed to check the building although there was no forced entry found. Just SOP. He handed me the key to the front door. I turned the key and opened the door.

I walked in, saw the "light panel" and switched the lights. Nothing. No lights. WT? Well, #$^&*. I would have to check the building with just my flashlight. I started at the front, working my way to the back. And then I saw it. In the middle of the floor. Nothing around it. Tools. Saws, hammers, paint cans. All stacked in a neat symmetrical pile. Hmm. But, okay. Then the glass racks. Standing on end. In the middle of the floor. Balanced it appeared. Wasn't gonna touch that. The little light at the back suddenly stopped "flickering". I walked on. And as I walked, I swear I could hear voices. Barely perceptible but distinct. I stood, looking around. Nope. Just me in there. I made my way back to the back door and gave it another little pull, Locked. So, no forced entry. I turned to walk back toward the front and as I turned, I saw a figure. Well, not so much a figure as a *shadow*. But, a transparent shadow. I admit, it startled me for a second. And then it was gone. Just gone. I had a chill run through me. I shook it off. Whatever was going on my job here was done.

I walked back through the dark building. Past the glass racks standing on end, past the stacked tools. I walked out the front door, told the owner there had been no intruders. He grumbled some more and I walked back to my patrol car and got in. I sat for minute. What had I just seen and heard? No idea. But, didn't want to go back there again.

Time passed. I would drive by that old building once in a while. The owner never finished the renovation. It now sat empty. With whatever or whoever it had inside ...

CANYON DRIVE

I knocked on the front door of the Church Rectory. Presently Father Henry opened the door and stepped aside and said, "Ah, Sergeant. Thank you for coming." I walked in the door to the Rectory proper. Had never been there. Very neat. Clean. Smelled a slight odor of incense.

Father Henry was, how should I say ... *portly*. Short and round. His frock was a little tight on him. Had been Father here for only a few months. Maybe 70 years old. Thick gray hair combed back. Pale complexion. Father didn't get out in the hot West Texas sun much. Didn't blame him. His small brass rimmed glasses down on his nose. He had called and asked me to drop by. Hoped he didn't want to save my soul. That could go in several directions.

He ushered me into the small kitchen. Motioned me to have a seat at the old wooden table. I sat. He asked, "Want a *cuppa?*" I did. I like coffee. He poured a cup for me and a cup for him and he sat across the table from me.

"I wanted to ask you about the house at the dead end of Canyon Drive," he said. *Ohhh.* That house.

"What would you like to know, Father," I asked.

He said, " I heard there was a tragedy there." I answered, "Yes, sir." I didn't elaborate. Not till I found out where this was going. "Death at the house?" He asked. Okay. I would tell him. Some of it. I said, "There was a murder-suicide at that house." He took a sip of his coffee, leaned back in his chair and said, "A violent death in that house. I was afraid of that." And he told me about the house on Canyon Drive ...

The coffee was good. Black and strong. I sipped my cup as Father Henry continued.

"One of my Congregation, Mister Fuller, owns that house on Canyon Drive. He has owned the house for a long time and rented it out and he has asked me to *bless* it." Farther continued. "He said that since an incident had happened there, he couldn't rent the house for any length of time. Renters would move out after only a couple of weeks. He told me renters related that they would hear shouting, see shadows, be touched ... even growls. He was hesitant to say what the *incident* was but he finally told me that there had been deaths in the house. He asked me if I would bless the house and that I should call you to explain what had happened there."

I leaned back in my chair. Okay. I would tell him some of it. No *details*. It had been a bad scene.

It had been two years ago. The Johnsons had lived there. Bad news. Both of them. Dopers. Middle aged couple. They would pop some meth, toke a little bud ... and fight. Violent fights. We (Deputies) would make calls there when the neighbors called because of the yelling and screaming. I had arrested Harold Johnson a few times. Domestic violence. Assault. Mary Johnson would refuse to press charges and he would be released and go back home and start again. Then that hot August night I had responded to a "shots fired" call at the Johnson house. I had found them both dead on the living room floor. Mary Johnson shot in the head. Harold lying beside her with a Glock .40 in his right hand and a hole in his head. Long investigation. Myself, Coroner, CSI all involved. End result— Harold had shot Mary and then turned the gun on himself.

I related that to Father and he listened intently. Then said, "Will you take me to the house? I fear that I may need someone with me when I do the *blessing*. I really don't want to do that alone."

I thought about it a moment. And said "Sure." I would take him to the house. We rode in silence for a awhile, and then I asked Father, "Why do you need me, Father? Don't know that I can be of much use to you." Silence ... then he said, "Because I suspect the worst. Demons ..."

The house on Canyon Drive. Dead end of a cul-de-sac. Fairly nice neighborhood. Usually pretty quiet. I pulled up out front of the house and parked. The house needed some paint. Yard needed mowing. The sun was setting in the West Texas sky. A purple hue was prominent. Pretty sunset. But most sunsets out here were nice. Father Henry looked over at the house. Didn't say anything. Just looked at the house. I didn't say anything. Father Henry was lost in thought and I didn't want to disturb him. He finally opened the door and stepped out of the car and walked through the fence gate toward the house. I followed.

We stepped up on the porch and Father bent down and with a key unlocked the door. I stood behind him. He opened the door. And just stood there looking in. Then he took a deep breath and stepped in. I followed.

The house was empty. No furniture. Nothing but walls. He stood in the living room. Odd, I thought. Ninety degrees outside and the house had a chill. I immediately looked down at the living room floor. Where I had found Harold and Mary. Both dead. A dark stain on the wood floor. Father never said a word. He breathed heavily. Then he said, "You might want to just wait here till I finish. I've only encountered what I believe is here one time before. I was praying I would never have to do such as this again."

He walked away down the hall. I stood there alone. No sooner had he walked out of sight and I heard a slight *moan*. Yup. I heard it. I looked around. Nothing. Okay. My imagination. Then a door slammed somewhere. I admit I was startled and jumped at the sound. I walked toward the kitchen. As I walked in a cabinet door opened and shut. I stared. WTF? Then footsteps behind me. I turned to see nobody. Okay. Enough of this *&^&*! But what was I supposed to do? So, I walked back in the living room. I could hear Father Henry in the distance. Toward back of the house. Talking. To who I couldn't imagine. Then very clearly a word. One word. *LEAVE*. Whatever was going on here they hadn't prepared me for this at the Police Academy. Then a gust of cold wind. In a closed house. Then it happened. I was touched. A hand across my back. I heard Father Henry shouting as he went walking from room to room. Well, I wasn't about to stay where I was after the things that had happened! I walked rapidly down the hall and found Father Henry in a bedroom. He was leaning back into a window sill. Pale. Holding a small silver crucifix in his hand. He was sweating profusely. "Father", are you okay?" I asked. He breathed heavily. "I've done all I can do. There are two of them. Demons. Angry!" He said. And then a low *growl*. "We must leave now," he said. He heaved himself off of the window seal and paced toward the bedroom door. Me on his heels. Straight through the living room and out the front door!

We sat in my patrol car. Silent. I was perplexed. Demons? Angry? What had I seen? What had I heard?

It was dark now and night enveloped us. Father said, "I don't think I was able to evict them. They are too powerful." I didn't know how to respond to that. So, I didn't. I started the car and drove away.

Time went by. The house on Canyon Drive stood empty. For years. No one wanted that house. And then one night ... a fire. Engulfed the old house and it collapsed in on itself.

I didn't speak about what Father and I had encountered that night. It would have felt wrong to do so. I could only hope that the *demons* had burned in that fire. If not ... I had no answers. The nights continued to be pretty at sunset in that little West Texas town. And life continued ... but I remember. I will always remember that house on Canyon Drive ...

THE TAYLOR HOUSE

The drive to the Taylor house was a short drive. Only a few blocks from the Courthouse. A neat ranch style little house. Well kept. I pulled in the driveway and parked. I sat for minute thinking how I was going to address her thinking that her deceased husband appeared in her room last night. Ghosts were not in my job description.

The Taylors were a well-respected family in town. George Taylor had been an insurance agent for years and Ms. Taylor was a retired school teacher. Last week she had been to an "art league" meeting with other ladies at the library, returned home to find George on the living room floor. Ambulance called, transported to hospital ... DOA at hospital. Autopsy indicated heart attack. Tragic, but just his time. He had been 64 years old. And how did I know this? Small town. Everybody knows everybody's business.

I got out of my car and walked up on the porch and knocked on the door. Ms Taylor opened the door immediately. Matronly looking lady. Gray hair. Short. I had met her a few times. Small town. She was dressed in a flower pattern dress. Old school. She looked a little "frazzled". Face pale, eyes red. "Oh, Sergeant come in ... come in", she said and stepped back from the door. "The Sheriff said he would send you over to help," she continued. I stepped into a neat, small living room. I said, "How can I help you, Ms. Taylor?" She elaborated, "Well, George was here last night." Not knowing how to respond to that I looked at her and mumbled, "Oh, really?" She said, "Yes." A statement. She was sure.

"Please come in my room", she said and walked toward the back of the house. Not having an option, I followed her. We walked into a bedroom. Bed made. Neat. A western style quilt cover. Nightstands on either side of the bed. Dresser, chest of drawers, mirror. Standard bedroom.

She turned and looked at me as we walked in, saying, "George was standing beside his side of the bed and pointing to his nightstand." Again, not knowing how to respond I just looked at her. "Yes, yes I know ... he's dead but he was here!" She said. The school teacher in her daring me to question her. Nope. Not gonna do that. And she stated her story ...

Ms. Taylor then related that she had went to bed and turned off the small nightstand lamp beside her bed. At this point she said she had seen him. Standing on the other side of the bed. Slightly *transparent* but it was George. Wearing the blue dress pants and white shirt that he had been wearing when she had returned to find him on the livingroom floor. She had looked at him, not afraid. It was George. Her husband for nearly 50 years. She called to him but he didn't answer. He just started pointing to the nightstand by his side of the bed. He had seemed insistent— vigorously pointing at the nightstand! She had asked him "what he wanted?" He had continued pointing to the nightstand. Repeatedly! She then reached over and turned on the lamp on her nightstand. He had vanished. Just gone.

She had slept fitfully last night and this morning she arose from bed and walked over to the other side of the bed to George's little nightstand. A little one drawer affair. She had reached down and tried to open the drawer. No luck. She had never looked in the drawer. No real reason to. When she couldn't get it open, she had called the Sheriff. He was a personal friend, and had always been there for the both of them should they needed any help with anything. And he had told her he would send me over. And over I was.

"Can you open that drawer for me?" She asked. Okay. Sure. I leaned over and pulled on the drawer. Stuck. Wouldn't open. I pulled harder. Nope. Not happening. She walked closer to me and said, "Will this help?" I looked to see a small screwdriver in her hand. Okay. Maybe. I took the screwdriver and leaned over and started prying around the little drawer. I pried and pulled, feeling the drawer give some, and then I jerked hard and open it came! I stood up straight and said, "Got it!" I glanced down in the drawer to see a small white envelope. "NORA" was written on the envelope. I stood back and Ms. Taylor leaned over and took it. She stood looking at it. Then looked at me and said, "I have a letter opener in the living room." And with that she turned and walked out of the bedroom leaving me standing there.

I stood ... just kinda looking around. Wondering. And the small lamp on the nightstand came on. WT? I looked at the lamp and it turned off. Then back on. Then back off. The overhead ceiling light came on. Then off. Then both the little lamp and ceiling light came on at the same time. Then off. Another WTF? I stood for a minute longer and turned and walked out of the bedroom to the living room where Ms. Taylor was sitting on the couch with the envelope and using the letter opener to open it. Okay. Mission accomplished. Drawer was opened and I gave Ms. Taylor my regards, she thanked me and I left.

Back at the Courthouse I told the Sheriff the results of my visit with Ms. Taylor. Minus the lights going on and off. No point in mentioning that.

It was the next day that the Sheriff told me that Ms. Taylor had called and said that the contents of the "envelope" was in fact a large life insurance policy for her. She would be financially secure for the rest of her life.

I had leaned back in my office chair and wondered. Had Mr. Taylor really appeared to her? What about those lights flashing on and off? Whatever had happened it was all good. I stood and took my tattered Stetson off my desk, adjusted my gun belt and left my office. I was *off-duty* and needed to go home and have a cold Bud Lite ...

REMEMBER THE ALAMO

So. I was an Alamo Ranger on the Alamo Complex in San Antonio for a number of years. Thousands of tourists and activity daily. But after we hustled the tourists and staff out and closed the gates in the evenings ... it was a different energy in the Complex. The sun went down and while the city bustled 'til way after midnight, the Alamo Complex was quiet. We would lock the Chapel doors, and without fail as we did so we would hear low, distinct *voices*. Never could make out the words themselves ... except once. I was alone and had closed and locked the front Chapel door and had set the alarm, and as I was exiting the rear doors, I heard ... "The north wall ... the north wall!" The voice was low and frantic. I finished locking the doors and walked out. Shadow figures late at night along the Long Barracks. Walking. On some nights we could hear a *fiddle* being played. We Rangers never really talked about those things. Just kind of accepted it. It is what it is. "Some" were still there. Paranormal? Absolutely. So late at night on the Complex ... they are still fighting the battle that would forever define Texas. I have seen and heard them. Remember the Alamo ...

This is one of the first drawings depicting the Misión San Antonio de Valero (The Alamo), created in 1838 by Mary Maverick.

THE MAID

High end. High end homes, yards, cars. Money. Lots of it.
The call had been simple enough. Lady had told Dispatch that
she was hearing "things" in her home. She wasn't frightened.
Didn't feel in danger. Just thought someone was in her home
with her. About 2:30 in the afternoon on a beautiful, sunny
day. The long, tree lined driveway wound around to a nice
two-story English Tudor.   I parked next to a Lincoln
Navigator. I got out of my patrol car, walked up on the long
front patio to the door and rang the doorbell. The door opened
to reveal an older lady wearing a nice dress holding a little
"ankle-biter" in her arms. She had *do-dads* on— a necklace,
and bracelets on her wrists. They sparkled and I was betting
that they weren't glass. I walked into a foyer with a spiral
staircase on the right. A big chandelier hanging from the
ceiling. I introduced myself and asked how I could be of
service. She related she had been out to lunch with friends
and returned home and had been "hearing things" in the

house. Just things sounding like they were being moved around, doors opening and closing.

Okay. I told her I would check the house, and I started downstairs first. Foyer, dining room, office area. Walking through the kitchen I saw a lady standing with her back to me at the sink. She turned to face me when I walked in. Short lady. Portly. Wearing a gray dress, white apron and one of those little white "thingies" on her head. The maid. I asked her if she had heard or seen anything unusual. She said, "No, sir". I continued walking the downstairs. Nothing. I then climbed the spiral staircase to the second floor. Five bedrooms, bathrooms. Long carpeted hall. Nothing.

I walked back downstairs to find the lady of the house sitting on a crushed velvet looking couch, still holding the ankle-biter. I explained that I had checked the whole house and found no evidence of an intruder. She got a little indignant, insisting she had heard noises and doors opening and closing. I stood looking down at her on the couch wondering if she was on crack. She had probably heard the maid doing maid stuff. I explained that I had even asked her maid if she had heard or saw anything and she hadn't heard or saw anything unusual.

Now the lady was looking at me like I was the one on "crack" ...

I looked at her. She looked at me. "I don't have a maid," she said. What? *Yes, you do*, I thought. I turned and walked back to the kitchen. Maid wasn't there. Well, big house. She could be anywhere. I walked back to the parlor and the lady.

I wasn't inclined to go searching the whole house for the maid and I wasn't going to argue with the lady. I had checked the house and no intruders, and I was sure she had just heard the maid. So, I repeated that the house was secure and that she was in no danger.

I left. Told Dispatch I was 10-8 and went on to other business.

Not two hours later Dispatch got another call from the same lady. Same complaint. Okay. One more time! Pretty much the same as the first call. Noises. Doors opening and closing. I searched the house. I didn't see the maid this time but was sure she was somewhere. And the lady repeated. No maid. BS! I had not only seen her, I had talked to her! No boogers in the house. I explained that all was good. Lady was somewhat indignant. I was too. And I left ... again.

And just at shift change when I was supposed to be getting off ... BAM! Okay, by now my usual easy going cop self was *P*&^#$*D!* This time was going to be the last time! Enough! Money or no money, she just might be going to jail for abuse of 911.

At the house when she opened the door I went all *Bad Cop*— telling her about 911 Abuse. Told her it was the maid making the noises. She turned and walked back to her velvet couch with her ankle-biter. Me hot on her diamond covered self-heels!

She sat down on her velvet couch and took a deep breath and said, "Sergeant. You said you had seen the maid. Well, I have too. And that's the problem. Cassie, our maid ... died two weeks ago. There in the kitchen. Heart attack. Cassie had been with us over twenty years. We loved her. She was more than just a maid. She took care of us in so many ways. But, about a week ago I started seeing her. Here and there. She seemed to be going about her duties. She would always be at a distance. Not close enough for me say anything. At first, I was frightened. But, then the more I saw her the less anxious I became. But of course, I couldn't be seeing her. She was dead. And if I wasn't seeing her then someone must be here in the house with me. That's why I have been calling. I wasn't about to admit to myself that I had been seeing a *ghost*. And when you said that you had seen Cassie in the kitchen, I really thought maybe I wasn't losing my mind. What is going here, Sergeant?" And just then ... a door slammed shut. Somewhere in the house. Loud.

I looked back over my shoulder. Didn't see anything. Big house. That door being slammed could be coming from anywhere. I turned and starting walking the house. Nothing downstairs, I headed up the staircase. At the top of the landing and down at the end of the hall ... I swear I saw her! Cassie. The maid! She had walked out of one the bedrooms across the hall into another bedroom. WTF? Distance of about twenty yards between her and I. She had been somewhat *luminescent* but it was the maid! I boot scooted down the hall and into the bedroom she had walked into. Nothing! *Cassie* wasn't in there! But I had seen her! I started a systematic search— every room, every closet. Every bathroom. Nothing. I stood in the hall. A slight chill in the air.

Nothing left for me to do but go back downstairs. I had no idea what I was going to tell the lady. That I had seen a ghost? *Uhhh* ... no. I went back downstairs to the lady and her ankle-biting companion. I told her that I had checked the house again and no one was in the house. She sat looking up at me and a slight smile came on her face. "You saw her again ... didn't you? You don't have to say anything. The look on your face tells me you saw her," she said. I didn't know how to respond. So, I didn't. Just stood there. She continued, " But you're seeing her brings some peace to me. I know I'm not crazy and she just wants to stay here, being our maid." I told the lady that she was in no danger from any people in the house. Nobody was there. She just smiled and thanked me.

I sat outside in my patrol car, trying to wrap my head around what had just happened. Whatever it was ... *just was*. I realized that shift change had come and gone. I was now *off-duty*. Good. I needed to go home. A shot of JD and coke might help. It might ... but ...

THE DOLL

"A what?" I asked as I leaned back in my office chair. He repeated what I had thought he said. I didn't know quite how to respond to that. I thought for a moment and said "Okay, I'll be over shortly."

The drive to John Mendoza's house was on the far side of town. And as I drove the old Ford patrol car to his house, I couldn't help but wish that Dispatch had found somebody else to put his call through to. Why me? But it had been me, so away I went.

His voice on the phone had been strained. He had stuttered a little as he had talked. He sounded frightened. It was all about a *doll*. A small, cloth doll. With "pins" in it.

A doll with pins in it. He was convinced it was "black magic". Where was this going?

A "Voodoo Doll" ... Again, I thought ... Why me?

The neighborhood was middle class. Older homes but well-kept yards. Clean. Nice. The sun was threatening to set as I pulled up in front of Mr. Mendoza's home. It mirrored the rest of the neighborhood. Small, neat. A soft brown exterior. I didn't get out immediately. Sat in my old patrol car. Just sat, thinking. How was I going to help Mr. Mendoza. I mean ... it was just a "doll". Throw it in the trash. Well, I would just have to see what this was all about.

I got out of my car, adjusted my gun belt and walked up to his front door and knocked. The door swung opened immediately! I stepped back a little startled! Mr. Mendoza was a Hispanic gentleman, maybe mid 70's. Dressed in a blue sport shirt, blue jeans and nicely polished cowboy boots. Thinning gray hair. He said, "Come in, please." I stepped into a small livingroom. Again, very neat. Very clean. Couch, coffee table, recliner, two cushioned chairs, big screen TV and ... candles burning all around the room.

I stood in the middle of the room looking at the candles and the many crucifixes on the walls. Kinda creepy I thought. And in the middle of the floor a small paper bag and a doll lying next it. I looked at Mr. Mendoza and he related that he had heard a "knock" at his door and opened the door to find the paper bag, now on the floor, on his porch. He had picked the paper bag up, stepped back in his house, and closed the door. He opened the paper bag and suddenly had sharp stinging sensations all over his body! He had dropped the paper bag and the doll had tumbled out. The stinging sensations continued for a few minutes before stopping. He had then called the Sheriff's office to ask for help. Hence, my presence at his house.

I looked at Mr. Mendoza. He looked at me. I then looked down at the doll on the floor. About six inches in length. Crudely made. A hideous red "grin" painted on its face. Large red eyes. And "pins" stuck all over it. WT? I leaned over a little, looking at it. *Yup.* Nasty looking little thing. I looked back at Mr. Mendoza. He looked at me. "There's a *hex* on me now!" He exclaimed. A "hex"? *Uh-huh.* And just exactly what I supposed to do about a "hex"?

I looked back down at the "doll". Well, I had seen some kinda story one time on a travel channel about Voodoo stuff and it had shown a doll that looked kinda like one lying on the floor in front of me. Mr. Mendoza said, "I want it out of my house!" *Uh-Huh.* The insinuation being that he wanted ME to take the "doll". *Hmm.* Well, I didn't know about that. I didn't believe in "hexes" and Voodoo but I was getting bad vibes about that "doll".

And cops believe in vibes. So, I stood looking down at that damn "doll" and thinking "bad karma" with this thing. And what had started strange was about to get just weird.

So, I stood looking down at it. Not knowing what to say. But, that *$^&* doll was bad juju, I had no doubt. And being a cop I, as with any situation, I needed a *motive*—why had Mr. Mendoza been the recipient of that spawn of Satan?

So, I asked him. He related that he had recently been to New Orleans and had occasion to get into a fight with a Cajun. The wife of said Cajun had told him that he would suffer for what he had done to her husband. *Uh-Huh.* Now I was getting the picture. Louisiana culture I was familiar with. And Voodoo was a very prominent part of the Cajun culture.

So, what to do here? I could just pick the doll up and take it with me and toss it in the trash. But wasn't inclined to do so. Didn't want to even touch that thing. That crude red smile on its face was just creepy. It was getting dark by now and I was deliberating a solution ... every light in the house came on. Mr. Mendoza jumped and I stood just looking around. Lights on. Every room. *Uh-Huh.* Okay. Then a "growl". Distinct. Low and menacing. And it was at that point that Mr. Mendoza let out a little *screech* and abandoned ship ... as it were ... and out the door he ran.

Well, by now I was a little nervous myself. But I wasn't going to let a doll dictate my actions. Was I ...?

So, I stood looking down at that doll. Mr. Mendoza was gone— no idea where. Lights flickering. A soft "growl". I didn't want to touch that thing. But Mr. Mendoza had called for help. I had to do something. That hideous red grin looking up at me. I took a deep breath ... bent over and grabbed the sack in one hand and the doll in the other. The pins sticking my hand. Immediately a stinging sensation covered my body! I jerked and gritted my teeth. Lights flickering, doors started slamming in the house. My body stinging, I managed to stuff the doll in the paper sack. I turned and ran out the door. No sign of Mr. Mendoza. I sprinted to my patrol car, threw the sack in the back seat and sped off. Driving fast. Out of town. Sweating profusely as I drove. About five miles out of town on an old dirt road to nowhere I stopped. I grabbed the paper sack out of the back seat and walked out a ways and threw it on the ground. Fumbled in my pocket for my lighter, found it, bent over and lit the sack on fire! Immediately a loud "shriek" from the bag! I turned and boot scooted back to my patrol car and sped off. Leaving that monster burning!

I called Mr. Mendoza the next day. He was okay and thanked me for my help. I would never forget my brush with Voodoo. And hope that had been my last encounter with Louisiana witchery.

LIES

"Every mystery ... begins with a lie." Cops will tell you that about their job. And Ms. Hernandez had lied to me about what she had seen. I had to wonder why ...

Tamales. That's how I first met Ms. Hernandez. The best homemade tamales in San Antonio. She sold them out of her small, modest home on the south side. She didn't advertise— just word of mouth to a small select group. I had been going by her home once or even twice a week for her pork tamales. For years. Nice lady. A real sweetheart. So, when she had called me sounding nervous ... scared ... and asked if I could come to see her, I didn't hesitate. I beat cheeks over to house. My office was on the north side of San Antonio so the trip pushed about 45 minutes. My unmarked black Chevy Tahoe purring through the traffic.

Her house was on a side street off the 410 Loop. Early evening, and the summer sun was cooking. I pulled up out front of her house and parked. Neat little house. Yard immaculate. She loved working in her yard. I walked through the fence gate onto her porch and knocked. She immediately opened the door. She looked bad. Eyes red. Complexion pale. Her usually clean, starched white apron was wrinkled. Something was wrong.

She stood inside her door looking up at me and said, "Oh, sir ..." She always called me "sir" even after I had begged her to call me Bob many times. "... I'm sorry to have bothered you but I just thought that some things here were .... well, please ... never mind. I was wrong. Thank you for coming." And she closed the door leaving me standing outside. I stood for a minute wondering what was happening to Ms Hernandez. I turned and walked back to my Tahoe. Got in and drove down to the corner, turned around and parked watching her house. Something wrong. Very wrong. I wasn't about to leave her like that. She had lied to me. And I was going to find out why ...

I sat in my Tahoe for a long time. Just watching Ms. Hernandez's house. Nothing going on. Nobody came around. Well, enough. I eased down the street to her house and parked out front. Got out and went to her door and knocked. No answer. I knocked again. Was a few minutes and she opened the door. She still looked rough. Like she had been crying.

I said, "Ms. H can I come in?" She sighed and stepped back and I walked in her house. A place for everything and everything in its place. Not a speck of dust anywhere. Clean and neat. She said, "Have a seat," gesturing toward the large couch. I sit. "Ms. H, something is upsetting you? Is there anything I can do?" She sat down in her old wooden rocking chair across from me. "Oh, I'm just a silly old woman. Imagining things," she said. "Like what?" I asked. She shifted herself in her chair.

"Okay. It seems things here in the house ... they *move*. On their own. My glasses for instance. I can put them down and go to get them later and they're not where I left them. They will be on the bed or the dresser. Not where I left them on the nightstand. My kitchen things. Spoons, forks, knives. If I turn my back, they ... move. Sometimes just an inch and sometimes across the counter. My car keys I found in the bedroom closet! I didn't leave them there! I don't think I did. I may be losing my old mind."

She was embarrassed to be telling me these things. She hung her head down. Well, I certainly didn't think she was losing her mental faculties. Seemed as sharp as ever just two days ago when I had stopped by to get my tamales. So, something else was going on.

I sat, just kinda looking around. Wondering. Then I saw something I hadn't seen before. Ms. H loved knick-knacks. Had all kinds on shelves around her house. Bowls, little ceramic chickens, jars of marbles. Just knick-knacks. But there on a shelf I saw what looked like an old sword or saber. Broken blade, rusted hand guard. I had never seen that before. And I love history. Relics. Antiques. I got up from the couch and walked over to the shelf and leaned over for a closer look. Wow. Definitely an old saber. Rusted, and broken in-two but a saber for sure. And very old.

I turned to Ms. H and asked, "Ms. H. I've never seen this before. Where did you get this?" She shrugged her shoulders and said, "Oh. I found that old thing when I was digging in my garden out back." Lots of history here in San Antonio. I was fascinated looking at that old saber. I leaned over to pick it up and look at it more closely. I could swear that it seemed to move. Just a bit. I picked it up. Cold as ice. Seemed to *tingle* a little. I looked at it. Turning it over in my hands. Very old.

I held it by the hilt— that tingling sensation again. I didn't like the vibe I was getting from it. At all. "Ms. H when did you start noticing things moving around?" I asked. "Well, about a week ago I think it was," she said. "Before or after you found this saber," I asked. She didn't answer for minute. Thinking. "Seems that things started moving around the day after I found that thing if memory serves," she responded.

Bad karma from that old saber, I thought. I could feel it. "Ms. H would you mind if maybe I took this thing back out to your garden and reburied it?" I asked. "Well, no. Go ahead if you want to. It doesn't match any of the other knick-knacks I have anyway", she said.

I turned and started out through the kitchen to the back door. I wanted this thing out of her house. I was walking through the kitchen and the broom she kept in her kitchen fell from the corner across the back door. I didn't slow down. I stepped over the broom and out the back door. Straight to her tiny garden— picked up her shovel— dug a hole about two foot deep— put the saber in it and covered it up. Then I marched back in the house and told Ms. H she should move her gardening to the side of the house. She just said, "Okay." I gave her a hug and told her to call if the moving things continued. And left.

She didn't call and I stopped by a week later for my tamales. Nothing had moved since I took the saber away, she said. She hugged me.

Did that saber have anything with what had been going on with Ms. H? Don't really know. But whatever had been going on had stopped. And I got a dozen free tamales. A win-win for me ... I do love tamales ...

FANNIE

Thing is, about half way through my forty-year career of wearing a badge and gun I had went from "skeptic" to "skeptical believer" to "believer". Things I had seen had no other explanation than being ..."paranormal". So, I had just started accepting it for what it was. I have said before— it is what it is.

That's why as I was beating cheeks to a burglary call and had my old patrol car flying along on Procter Street and glanced Fannie Cariker in her yard I didn't flinch. Thing about that ... she'd been dead for a year.

Fannie was hadn't been well liked around town. TBT I didn't like her much either. A grouch. She was a widow who had moved to town and lived alone. Thin, wiry woman, gray hair in a bun. She would call the Sheriff's office about kids trespassing when they chased a ball from the street that had gotten away from them and had rolled into her yard. She called about loud kids, speeding cars, etc., etc. She was rude to her neighbors and snapped at anyone for any reason. She was out in her yard tending her flower garden a lot but never spoke to when someone tried to talk with her.

One day a neighbor had seen her laying by her flower garden. Ran to check on her and called an ambulance, but too late. She was DOA at the hospital. May seem cruel to say but she wasn't missed in the neighborhood. Or anywhere else around town for that matter.

So, when I started hearing rumors about "things" happening around her house and neighbors seeing "her" in her yard I wanted to stop that nonsense. Wasn't good for that kind of talk to be spread and scaring folks. But when I got into the bones of the rumors and talk, I was drawn into Fannie still being there ... a year after she died.

And so, after hearing the neighbors being insistent about seeing Fannie, long after she died, I found myself parked in front of her house. Well, what had been her house. A hot, scorching July day. The AC in my old patrol car whining ... trying to cool. I sat looking at the house. Now owned by the bank. A For Sale sign in the yard. Been for sale since Fannie died— no buyers. Needed paint and some repairs.

I got out of my car, shifted by gun belt and Glock .40 on my waist and walked up on the porch to the front door. I tried the front door. It opened. I walked in. Dark, dank. Smelled of cigarette smoke. Empty. I walked each room. Nothing. I stood in the living room. Suddenly ... a chill. Strange. I walked out to the yard, headed to my patrol car and stopped. Her garden. It was green. Flowers growing. Garden was neat. Neighbors must have been tending it. Couldn't imagine why.

I drove back to my office at the Sheriff's Department. Up to the second floor. I closed my office door and settled into my old leather desk chair. And being the old curious cop that am, I leaned forward and started pecking on my computer. I pulled up Fannies death certificate. Got her DOB and SS#. Then changed gears and went into the NCIC database. Wow. Fannie had indeed been a *widow*. To THREE different husbands! Her first husband had died of an *accidental gunshot* wound. Her second husband been ran over in the street. Car and driver had never been found by the local PD. Third husband had died if an *accidental overdose.* The PD in that town wasn't much convinced the overdose was "accidental" but the Grand Jury didn't return an indictment against Fannie. She walked away with a very good insurance settlement. Matter of fact she had walked away from all three dead husbands with a healthy insurance settlement. Fannie had moved here several years go. Alone. I leaned back in my old chair. The old wheels in my head turning. Would any of that have anything to do with the claims of the neighbors of having seeing Fannie. A year after she had died?

I stood up, grabbed my old Stetson off my desk. I was going back to Fannie's house. I needed an answer ...

Dusk. And for the second time that day I found myself parked in front of Fannie's house. The heat was oppressive. The AC in my old patrol car fighting a losing battle. Didn't really know what I was doing there. Like I said ... looking for answers. Were the neighbors really seeing Fannie? I got out of my car and made the short walk to the front door. I opened the door and stepped in.

The house was darker than before. But an "aura" seemed to fill the rooms. Something there. I was perplexed but intent on trying to make some sense of what was happening to upset the neighbors. I walked room to room. Empty. Nothing. I stood in the living room looking around and then ... heard a voice. More of a *whisper* really. "Leave." A whisper but ... demanding. And then ... a touch. On my back. At first just that. A touch. A shiver ran up me. I was startled, and stepped back. Then the voice again ..."LEAVE" ... this time louder! Demanding! Bad juju for sure. And then a "shove" in my back. At this point I was discombobulated and decided that Fannie or whatever was there wanted me out and I turned and walked toward the door. And ... saw her. Standing by the door. A *shadow* really but Fannie. I stopped cold! She was looking directly at me and then ... smiled. A cold, dark smile. And then she was ... gone. Just not there.

I boot scooted out the front door. Into the yard and stopped. I glanced back at the door. It closed. I got back in my car and sat for a moment. Trying to wrap my head around what had just happened. No luck with that. The last thing I saw as I drove away was Fannie's garden. Green and fresh. Flowers blooming. No rain for weeks and her garden was beautiful. Was she still tending her garden? Neighbors said she was. And now I believed them.

So, I had returned to Fannie's looking for answers. Got none. Just more questions. Nothing I could do, so I left. And once in a while when driving down Fannie's street I would see her. In her yard. I would just glance and keep driving. I had wanted closure. But it seemed Fannie wasn't ready to leave. No closure— yet. Not just yet ...

RANDOM CHOICE

It had been a random choice. The kind we all make a hundred times a day. I had been driving on Hwy 90, not going anywhere in particular. I had just wanted out of my office for a while. Get away from the complaints, reports, phone calls and such. I had just needed a break.

So, when I got to the intersection on 39th I didn't turn south. I turned north. Just a random choice. North on 39th ...

The traffic was light. A Saturday evening. Late. 39th Street narrowed to two lanes. I drove on. Not really paying attention to where I was going. Just driving. My Tahoe purred. Eventually I found myself easing into the hill country. 39th had turned into a narrow two-lane farm to market road.

The road wound around the hills and canyons, deep canyons in places, steep cliffs cut into the countryside. A sharp turn in the road and I saw the Guadalupe rolling through the canyon below. The road hugged the cliff. I saw a "lookout point" ahead. You can pull over off the road ... just park and take in the scenery. I eased over and parked. Just sat contemplating life, as it were. No traffic on the road interrupted my thoughts. I noticed a small trail that led down into the canyon in the distance. I stepped out of my Tahoe and adjusted my holster and Glock .40 on my blue jeans and walked toward the small trail.

As I was walking, I happened to remember this place. Had heard about it. Even seen a few old pictures. Locals would whisper about it. Not talking about this place openly but among themselves. Legends haunted this canyon. The locals called this place ... Diablo Canyon.

I stepped off the pavement of the overlook point and started down the trail. My Tony Llamas crunching the trail rock as I walked the steep, narrow trail down along the cliff face. I walked slowly. Footing a little risky. The trail wound along the cliff face for a good ways. Then I rounded a big boulder and there was the river, flowing with a gentle roar. Boulders and rocks of all sizes along the bank. I just took a breath and stood ... looking. Nice. Peaceful. Nearly night now. Twilight. In between daylight and night. As I stood there, I glanced across the 75 yards of river to the other side, and as my eyes wandered, I saw her.

She was standing by a small boulder. A little girl. Looked to be about 10 years old. Long dress. Long blond hair. Very pale. I squinted. Could barely make her out. Then she turned and looked directly at me and stretched her arm out and with her finger pointed to something upstream. I looked. Didn't see anything but the river, rocks, boulders. And then on the backside of one of the boulders I could make out what looked like to be remains of a chimney. Torn apart but could still see parts of it. Stones strewn around the ground. Part of an old, stone house for sure. I turned back to the little girl. She was still there. Pointing, aggressively, at the old stone house. What was she needing? I called to her— my voice nearly a yell across the river— and asked her if she need help. She didn't appear to say anything. Just kept pointing. I called again, telling her I would come to her. I took a quick glance back at the old stone house, then turned to tell her I was coming, but she was gone. Just not there. Gone. I stood looking. Called. Over and over. Nothing. Just the gentle roar of the river. Had I really seen her? It was getting darker. Maybe just some kind of trick of the light on the water. I stood and called again. Nothing.

I thought a moment longer and gave up on what had happened. Strange. I started back up the trail to my Tahoe. Perplexed. Just as I got to the top of the trail and the pavement of the "overlook" I saw the old man. He was leaning against the pipe fence of the overlook just looking down in the canyon. He turned and saw me. Older fella. Long gray beard and hair. Dressed in coveralls. I kind of gave him a slight nod of my head and kept walking toward my Tahoe. Then he suddenly stepped in front on me. I stepped back. Looking him straight in his old wrinkled face. He glanced down and saw the Gold Shield clipped on my belt next to my gun. "You a cop?" He asked. "Sorta", I said. No use trying to explain who I worked for. People had all kind of ideas about who I worked for and I wasn't in the mood to get into that conversation.

He looked at me a moment longer. Then asked, "You saw her, didn't you?" I didn't say anything. He continued, "She sometimes comes out about this time late in the evening. She was pointing down to the old stone house, wasn't she?" I grunted. Non-committal.

He smiled. "That's okay. People don't know or understand what they saw down there," he said. "She died down there at the old Carson place." And then he told me the legend ...

The old man turned and walked over to the fence railing of the "overlook" and leaned against it. Leaving me standing a piece from him. He continued. Matter of fact. A slow drawl. "You have to understand. Back in 1886 farms, ranches and homesteads here were few and far between. A lot of distance between neighbors. People didn't really get too far from their place. Just a once-a-month trip to town or maybe to Church on Sunday. And especially during winter they just didn't wander far. The Carsons had moved here from Arkansas. That much we do know. He had built his place on the far side of the river. Carson, his wife and two small children, A boy and girl. Hardscrabble life, trying to farm hereabouts. One cold March evening Caleb Kershaw had been down in the canyon looking to round up some strays that had got out of the pasture. The Kershaws had their place about ten miles upriver from the Carsons and seldom saw each other. Caleb was wanting to get the strays back as soon as he could. It was cold and night was falling, and his old horse was getting tired. He was riding on the far side of the river. He rounded the bend down there in the canyon and glanced across the river and saw the little Carson girl. She was pointing downstream toward their place. Caleb pulled the reins and stopped his horse. Caleb thought it strange she was just wearing what looked like a thin long dress. It was cold, and Caleb was wearing his thick wool overcoat and he was cold wearing that. He called to her. Asking what she was doing out and about without a coat? She didn't answer. Just stood pointing toward their place. Caleb couldn't see much of the Carson place downstream. Their homestead was behind the boulders and trees. Caleb called to the girl again. Asking if she was okay? No response other than pointing toward their place downstream. Caleb decided he best go check on the girl. At least go by the Carson place and tell them that their girl was out without warm clothes. The nearest river crossing was about a mile downstream and Caleb wasn't looking forward to it. That river water was going to be damn cold. But something wasn't right with that little Carson girl. He called across the river to her and told her he was coming across and rode toward the crossing. The river was cold as he crossed and his horse sure didn't like it but he made it across. Back upstream he rode toward the Carson place. In a bit he rode up and noticed there was no smoke coming from the chimney. That was strange as hell as cold as it was. He dismounted and waked to the door. Knocked. Nothing. He pushed on the door. It opened. And a hellish scene confronted him. The house was torn all to hell! And lying on the floor ... the Carson family. All dead! Blood everywhere! And in the middle of the floor lay the little girl. The little girl he had just seen ..."

Night had fully fallen now, and in the moonlight the old man stopped talking and took a pack of cigarettes out of his overall pocket. Took one out of the pack and lit it. He took a long drag of the smoke and leaned back further on the fence rail. And continued ...

"Caleb stood taking in the horror. Carson, his wife, the boy... and the girl. All on the floor not only dead but from the look of the bodies they had all been dead for, Caleb guessed, at least a week! But he had just seen the little girl! Not an hour earlier! Down by the river! The house had been ransacked. Contents scattered all over. Caleb walked closer and could see bullet holes in all the victims. He turned and ran out, mounted his horse and galloped toward the Henderson ranch about five miles north. The cold north wind biting him. Long story short when he got to the Hendersons some of the ranch hands returned with Caleb to the Carson place and two other cowboys went after the Sheriff."

It was the next day after the Sheriff and two Deputies had come and took in the mayhem that Caleb and several other cowboys took the bodies out and loaded them in a flatbed wagon and took them to the church cemetery for burying. The town Doc had took a look at the bodies and said, "Yeah, been dead at least a week. Everybody thereabouts had turned out for the funerals."

"The Sheriff talked to everybody for miles around. No tracks around the Carson place to be followed. Wasn't Indians. Hadn't been Indian trouble around here for a long time. What few that were left were peaceable. Just hardcase outlaws? Marauders from Mexico? Time went by. Nothing to speak of about who had done that. Weeks, months ... years. No suspects in that murderous rampage. Caleb never said anything about seeing the little girl that day. She had been wearing the dress Caleb had found her in when he had seen her out by the river. But time eased by and he would tell a few folks about seeing her. Around the fireplaces and campfires folks began to say that only a *devil* could have done those murders. Folks avoided the canyon. But the few that found themselves passing through would whisper that they had seen the "little Carson girl" on the other side of the river. Pointing toward the Carson place. Always about sunset. And because people were convinced that the devil had done those murders that canyon was called Diablo Canyon. People around here say that they still see that little girl about sunset down there. By the river."

With that he stopped talking. Empty of words. He stood straight and said, "Nice to meet 'ya".... and turned and walked to the trail head on the far end of the "overlook". I called after him, "I didn't catch your name." He continued walking just down the trail down to the river but turned and said, "Lester ... Lester Kershaw."

Kershaw? The same name as Caleb Kershaw.

I stood watching him as he walked out of sight down the trail to the river. The night was dark. No moon. Nothing left for me to do. I walked toward my Tahoe. Had I really seen that little Carson girl? I decided I had. Her little soul forever destined to pointing to her family.

I drove away leaving Diablo Canyon. Leaving her ...

THE WEEPING

I had heard the legends. Most everyone in those parts had.
But I had driven past that old burned relic of a house a
hundred times. Never heard anything.

But that night I did hear it. The *weeping* ...

I had left a wreck scene out on the west end of the county.
It was late. I was tired. My old patrol car humming on the
lonesome, dark, two-lane black top. And as I drove past the
house, I heard it. Not exactly crying. Low, moaning. It was
"weeping". The sound was around me. I slowed and stopped,
trying to figure what I was hearing. I glanced over at the old
burned ruins of that house. It sat back off the road a piece.
Just a few charred stone walls. Burned cross timbers. Parts of
the roof had caved in. Full moon. I could see the old place in
the moonlight. Like I said, I had passed this place a hundred
times. No sounds around. Just a deserted, old, burned house.
No neighbors for miles. I sat in my car in the road. Weeping
was what I heard. Not crying. Then it stopped. No sounds
but the wind that always blew out here.   Maybe my

imagination but I was reminded of the legend people spoke about. Of people saying that the house wept. It could be heard weeping when people would drive past at night.

I didn't know much about the house. Had been abandoned ever since I had been here and had been that way for many years I had been told. I decided to do a little research. What had happened there? I wanted to find out.

I drove on through the dark night ...

The next morning, I got lucky. So, to speak. I walked into Kathy's for breakfast and saw Matt Hastings sitting at a table. Matt was the Chief of the Volunteer Fire Department. I had planned on going by the FD to talk to him anyway and this way I could have my biscuits, gravy and coffee and talk to him too.

I sat down at his table, shook hands and asked him about the old burned house and the "weeping" legend. He leaned back in his chair, sighed and said, "Wow. That was way before my time. That house burned way back in the early sixties, I think. I heard that a man, his wife and two kids were burned to death in that fire but I don't really know. And yeah, I've heard the legend. The house *weeping*. And I have to admit that one night I was coming back home from Angelo and drove by that house and thought I heard something. Not crying. More like that weeping people talk about. But figured it was just my imagination. But I tell you who could tell you about that house and the night it burned. Clive Howell. He's about the only one I know of who could tell you. He's got to be in his eighties now but he was a volunteer in the fire department back then. But, know this. Clive is somewhat of a recluse. Not the sociable type. But you can try." With that Matt gave me Clive Howells address, and after I had finished my biscuits, gravy and coffee and set out to talk to Clive Howell.

I found Clive Howells house easy enough. Neat tree lined street. Nice small house. I parked my old patrol car and got out and walked up to the door and knocked. No response. I knocked louder. This time the door was jerked open. A small, frail looking guy. Big stock of gray hair mussed up. Wearing a long bathrobe. I looked at him and said, "Mr. Howell, I'm Sergeant Dean with the Sheriff's Department and I was wondering if I could talk to you a minute about that old burned house out on Route 62?" He looked at me and said, "NO!" and slammed the door. I jumped back a bit as the door slammed. Damn! Oookay. So much for that. I went back to my patrol car and left for my office.

I had no sooner walked in my office and the phone rang. I answered, "Sergeant Dean, Criminal Investigation Division." The voice on the other end said, "July, 12th, 1962. 8:35 PM. Full moon. Four dead. Man, woman and two kids. Burned in the house. And yes. The damned house *weeps*. You can come over if you like your coffee black and strong." And the phone went dead.

And so, I went to see Clive Howell to learn about the Weeping House ...

I knocked on Clive Howells door hoping he hadn't changed his mind and slam the door in my face again. He opened the door. This time wearing clothes. Old pair of blue jeans and a dirty t-shirt. He didn't say anything. Just stood aside so I could walk in. I did. The room was dingy. Old furniture. Smelled of cigarette smoke. Ashtray beside the old couch full. He just motioned toward the couch and walked out of the room. I took a seatt on the couch. Returning with two steaming cups of black coffee. Handed me one and he took a seat at the opposite end of the couch. He took a pack of smokes out of his pants pocket, lit one, and leaned back and looked at me.

"You heard it didn't you?" He said.

I looked at him and said, "Heard what, sir?"

"You heard that damn house crying or weeping or whatever it does!"

I said, "Well, I heard something."

"It was a full moon last night and that's when it does it!"

I didn't take the bait. Not going to affirm I heard any such thing.

"I haven't talked about that night in a long time," he said.

"You were very specific about that house. The night it burned. Date, time, even a full moon."

"I know. It was bad, very bad. Just don't forget that kinda stuff," he replied. And then he began ...

"I was just a kid. Nineteen or so. That night us Volunteers responded to the fire department when the siren went off. When we got out there to that house it was in full bloom. Nothing much we could do. The Flanagan's house. He was a truck driver, married with a couple of kids. We didn't see anybody around the house and the car was parked out front. We figured they might all be in the house but no way we could get too close to see. We watered as best we could but the house was gone. Two hours just throwing water on it! Finally, we got it down to smolders and tried to look and see in the smoking inside. We couldn't make anything out. We stayed the whole night just making sure it didn't catch again. The next day the ME from Austin got there. He had a team with him. At the end of the day, he had found 'em. What was left of 'em. All four. Pretty soon the rumors started. Everybody knew the wife, Sissy Flanagan, had just got out of the nut house. Strange woman. In and out of the nut house. We could never find a direct cause of the fire. We didn't have all the fancy equipment they have now to figure out what and how fires started. And people started saying Sissy Flanagan had finally just went off the deep end and started the fire herself. Hell, we never found out one way or another. But then people started saying that on full moons driving by that damned house you could hear the thing crying or weeping or whatever. Nonsense I thought. Until I was out that way and just happened to be driving by on a full moon night and heard it. *Weeping.* I HEARD IT I TELL YOU! SCARED THE HELL OUTTA ME! And that's all I got to say about that damned house! You can leave now I got things to do." He got up off the couch and opened the door. I thanked him and left.

But I couldn't wrap my head around everything he had told me. Something just didn't make sense.

When I left his house, I turned out of town. Out on Highway 62— toward the Weeping House.

It was late evening by the time I got to the house. Narrow dirt drive. Grown over with grass and weeds. House a burned relic. Timbers here and there. All charred. Walls and roof partially collapsed. I parked my old patrol car. Got out and just started walking around the ruins. Weeds and burned wood. I kicked around. Nothing much here. I walked into what must have been the kitchen. Burned, rusted stove and fridge. I kicked around there awhile and started to leave. And then I happened to glance at the old rusted stove. Noticed something. I walked behind the stove. A brass fitting. It was broken off what must have been the gas line to the stove. I smiled. That might have caused the fire! A broken gas line! Not Sissy Flanagan.

The next day I returned to the house with the State Fire Marshal. Told him what I had found and pointed it out. He nodded his head. "Oh, yeah! That could have started a fire if there was an open fire on the stove." He wrote it all up as "accidental".

That evening I called Harry Taylor. Junk dealer in town. He met me at the house with a couple of guys and a truck. I told him to load the old stove and fridge and get them out. He did.

And then it stopped. No one heard the *weeping* from the house anymore on full moon nights. I figured that the house was weeping because Sissy Flanagan had been blamed for intentionally setting the fire. Killing her family. And now I had found out different. Not Sissy's fault at all. She didn't kill her family.

The house sat out there for many years after I did what I did. Did I have anything to do with the house not weeping anymore. Hell, I don't know about that. What I do know is that the house could rest now. Sissy wasn't a killer. She was not to blame and the house didn't weep anymore. Sometimes it's the innocent that get the blame. But not anymore at the Weeping House. Not anymore ...

THE CAR

It's a nasty, disgusting, filthy, dangerous habit. But it helps me with stress. Smoking. And if I hadn't stepped outside my office that night to smoke ... I wouldn't have seen it.

Clear night. Full moon. Warm. I stood on the sidewalk behind the Courthouse and lit my cigarette. The street was empty. A street light on across the street on the corner. Not late. About 9 o'clock. I leaned back against the building and smoked. A car approaching. A small car. Maybe a Toyota or Mazda. Light color. Gray? Two-door. It stopped at the stop sign in front of me on the street. I smoked. I glanced at the car. WT? I squinted my eyes. It was empty. No driver. No one in the car. WT? The car was maybe twenty-five feet in front of me stopped at the stop sign. Then it accelerated slowly and drove up the street. Again WT? Full moon. Street light. I could see in the car and ... ? *Humph.* Well, just the light or maybe I was just tired.

I took a last drag on my smoke, flicked it out to the storm drain and ambled back into my office. I sat in my old, leather chair trying to get back to the after-action reports on my desk that were due tomorrow at the DA's office. But it nagged at me. The car. I couldn't shake what I had seen. Or rather what I hadn't seen. No driver in the car. And then I remembered. The stack of nightly reports from the guys on my desk. I grabbed the stack and started sifting through them. And there, near the bottom I found them. I had read through the reports when I had got to my office and remembered three reports that I hadn't paid much attention to. Just nothing but people's imaginations or something. But I re-read the reports. People had called the past few nights, reporting a car without a driver. Driving through town. At night. No description except a small car and a light color. The deputies had done the obligatory check around ... finding no such car and made a short report. Also, I remembered a report from last week that a car had been stolen from the local junkyard. A Toyota. The junkyard owner wasn't too worried about it. Just felt he had to report it. Why anyone would want to steal it he couldn't imagine. It didn't even have a motor and the junkyard owner was perplexed on how whoever stole it had managed to get it out the gate. Strange.

I made a note on my desk calendar to go talk to the junkyard owner the next day. Probably no relation to what I had seen or what had been reported, but cop that I am, I was curious. A car. No driver. Stolen car matching the description but no motor to be driven around anyway. *Humph* ... but I hated loose ends so ...

The day dawned cloudy and cold. I stopped at Kathy's Cafe and got breakfast, then headed over to Fred's Junkyard. That damn car I saw last night was still on my mind. Fred had been in business with junk cars for years. His junkyard was on the far, south side. I drove up just as he was opening his gate.

Fred was an amiable guy and his overalls fit tight. Bald and chubby. He greeted me with, "Mornin', Sergeant. You're up early." I parked my old patrol car and walked in his shack he used for an office. He poured us both a cup of strong black coffee from the old pot and we both settled in on an old broken-down couch. I told him I was there about the car he had reported stolen awhile back. He laughed and said, "Don't tell me you found that junker?" I told him no but I might have seen it. I asked him to tell me about that car.

He took a sip of his coffee and said, "Strange stuff about that car. What I do know about it is that it belonged to a lady named Murphy. Widow woman. She bought it new. Loved that car, I'm told. Had it for years. 'Bout a year ago she took sick. Got bad. She didn't get out much. Her son would go by and see her. Try to take care of her. Finally had to put her in a home. You know, for old folks. The son didn't do anything with the car. Just left it in the driveway at her house. Then he went by her house just to check on stuff and the car was gone. He knew the keys were in the house on his mom's nightstand. He went in and checked. And, yeah. The keys were there. He called and reported it stolen. Cops came and took a report. He left and went to visit his mom at the old-folks home and be damned if that old car wasn't parked in the parking lot at the old-folks home! He couldn't figure what was going on! Just parked there. He asked around to staff there and nobody had seen it drive in or anything. Nothing damaged on the car. Just old and kinda beat up. The ignition hadn't been tampered with or anything. How did that car get there? The keys were back at his mom's house. He had just seen them there!"

Fred stopped talking and got the old pot and poured us another cup of coffee. Sat back down and said, "Then things really got strange with that old car ..."

Fred sipped his coffee, sighed and continued. "He called his wife and had her go to Ms. Murphy's, get the car keys off the nightstand and bring the keys to him. At the old-folks home he waited till his wife got there with his mom's car keys. When she got there, he got in the car, started it and drove it to his house. Once at his house he parked the car in his driveway, locked it and took the keys inside and put them in his nightstand drawer. Well, a couple of days later he went out to go to work. And the car was gone! He went back inside and checked. The keys were still in his nightstand! He called the Cops again, reported it stolen and went to work. On his way home from his job, he stopped by the old-folks home to visit his mom and there it was! His mom's car parked at the old-folks home! Again, he checked the car. Nothing. Ignition not tampered with. Nothing. Again, had his wife bring him the keys from his house. This time, though, when he went in to visit his mom, Ms. Murphy, he asked her about the car. But she was not really coherent. When he tried to talk about her car she could only smile and nod her head. Long story short, that happened three more times. He was frustrated. The old car wasn't worth much so he called me. I went and looked at it and gave him a few bucks for it. I could use it for parts. Had it towed here and here it's been. Sometimes. Found it missing four or five times. Cops made reports. It would turn up at the old-folks home. I would get it back here again. Finally took the motor out! That would stop that BS! I thought. By now you know better. I just don't pay attention anymore. It turns up missing and then at the old-folks home. No motor in it. And I hear people say they have seen it around town. No driver. Just driving. But I'm hoping that's over now. Ms. Murphy died last week. No reason for that damned car to end up at the old-folks home anymore. But yesterday it went missing again. I went by the old-folks home and it wasn't there. No idea where it's at now."

Fred ended his story. I thought for a moment, thanked him, and left. I had a hunch ...

I found the car. Where I thought it might be. It sat where I found it for years. Fred didn't want it. The car was parked out of the way. No hazard. Now just a rusting hulk. I think to this day what's left of it is still there ... with Ms. Murphy. At the cemetery.

THE DEATH HORSE

I had been on a routine theft call out at the Sullivan Ranch. Theft of a saddle and some spurs. Sounded like it was going to be a hired hand that had been fired a few days before. I would get into it tomorrow. It had been a long day.

I was about 10 miles out on a lonely stretch of two-lane blacktop headed back into town. About dusk. I turned onto Spring Canyon Road and just as I turned, I glimpsed a horse up on the mesa. Standing in the fading light of the day. Nothing unusual about seeing horses out here. But, up on that Mesa. In the distance. At dusk. It kinda gave me a chill. As if it was foreboding something.

I drove on through the twilight of the fading day ...

By the time I got back into town I was whupped. Bone tired. I had been at it close to fourteen hours. So, I went straight home and crashed.

The morning found me at my office going through the reports from the previous night. My guys had been busy. This and that. And then toward the bottom was a short incident report.   One of my guys had responded with the EMS ambulance out to the Sullivan Ranch. Old man Tom Sullivan, the ranch owner, had collapsed and died in the barn at the ranch. No foul play suspected. Looked like a heart attack. *Wow.* I had just talked to him yesterday, about the theft at his ranch. Good guy. Had known him for years. I thought for a moment and decided I should go out to the ranch and pay respects to Ms. Sullivan and see if she needed anything. I stood up, straightened my gun belt and Glock .40, grabbed my old Stetson hat off my desk, and headed out.

Cloudy day, rain maybe coming. Had heard that a blue-tailed norther was headed our way. As expected, when I drove into the ranch it was quiet. None of the ranch hands out and about. Nothing going on. I parked and walked up on the wide veranda and knocked on the door. Beautiful old home. Two story. Wide columns. Presently one of the ranch hands opened the door— Jerry was his name. Had been with the Sullivans on the ranch a long time. He said the Missus was in the living room and I could go right in. I walked in, down the hall, past the stairs to the living room. Large, expansive room. Furnished with antiques. I found Ms. Sullivan sitting on the couch, sipping a cup of coffee. Eyes red. Refined lady. Wearing a pair of blue jeans, a blue blouse and her cowgirl boots. She looked up and saw me, thanked me for coming. I expressed my condolences and offered any assistance she may need, etc. Then she *sighed* and said, "He knew it was coming. Told me he had seen the *Pale Horse* down in the draw behind the house." Pale horse? She must have seen the look on my face, because she explained, "The Pale Horse is seen around these parts foretelling a death. He told me he was going to die soon. That was two days ago. His younger brother saw the Pale Horse too just before he died of a snake bite years ago. And Jason Patterson died when he was thrown off his horse. Broken neck. He said the Pale Horse had ran past his house. The next day he was dead. Just because you see the Pale Horse doesn't mean you're going to die. But it means somebody is for sure." Not knowing how to respond I just gave a slight nod of my head. We talked a few more minutes. I then excused myself. And went out the door, started my old patrol car and left.

The cold was fast approaching. Could see the dark blue clouds on the horizon. I drove, and remembered. The horse I had seen up on the mesa the night before. Could that have been the *Pale Horse*? Too far away for me to make any colors but I did wonder. So instead of heading back to town I turned at an old two-lane dirt road. I was out this way so why not stop for a visit with Little Hawk— an old Apache Indian who had a hardscrabble ranch way back in a dead-end canyon. He and I got along well and he always had a pot of coffee on. If anyone knew about anything it was Little Hawk. Had he ever heard of the Pale horse? I was about to find out ...

The two-lane dirt road was rough. Shaking my old patrol car. Little Hawk's ranch, such as it was, was about five miles out in the middle of the nowhere. In the back of a small box canyon. I could see the norther coming in my rear-view mirror. Dark, blue clouds. Drove up in front of Little Hawk's house. Really wasn't much of a house. More like a two-room shack. The small old barn falling down, the corral had two Mustang ponies. Nothing around for miles. Just dirt, rocks and the canyon walls. I could see smoke coming from the smoke stack. I parked and sat, didn't get out. He knew I was here. When he was ready for me to come in, he would open the front door. So, I sat and waited. Ten ... fifteen minutes. Then the front door opened. He stood in the door. Little Hawk was maybe in his eighties. Gray hair pulled back in a long ponytail. Deep creases in his red face. Bent at the hips. Old worn blue jeans. Faded gray shirt. Old cowboy boots. I got out of my car and walked to the door. He gave me a slight nod and said, "Sergeant, I put a fresh pot on." A fresh pot. He had known I was coming? How? No idea. He just did. I stepped in the small room. Neat, clean. Small worn couch. Two old broken down recliner chairs. A wooden table used for meals, coffee and such. The old wood burning stove in the corner did indeed have a pot of coffee brewing. I could smell it. Chicory. Strong coffee. I sat down in a rickety old chair at the table. He poured two cups of steaming coffee, placed one in front of me and he sat down in a chair opposite me. We said nothing. Just sipped our coffee, Little Hawk would speak when he was ready. Not before.

Time passed. We sipped our coffee. He finally leaned back in his chair and said, "You saw it. The pale horse. The *Death Horse*."

I said nothing.

He *sighed*. "I will tell you ..." And he did ...

The norther was on us now. Could hear the wind outside howl. Little Hawk's expression was impassive. I sipped my coffee as he continued.

"Our forefathers lived here in the canyon. Chief Blue Sky lead our people then. He was a good leader for our people. He had a Mustang pony that he had raised since birth. It is said that the pony was *pale* white in color. He was called Blanco by the people. The pony was devoted to Blue Sky. Blue Sky led our people for many years. And when he passed on a winter's day our people were saddened. The pony seemed to know when Blue Sky passed and tore from his tether and ran to Blue Sky's lodge. He stood for hours outside as the people prepared Blue Sky for his final journey. Many tried to lead the pony away, back to be tethered. He would jerk away. Would not be lead away from Blue Sky. He followed the people with Blue Sky to the end of this canyon and watched as Blue Sky was released to the heavens. After the ceremony Blanco ran away, to the plains and canyons here. He was seen by the people, always at a distance, before a death in our tribe. Always at twilight. The people feared his sighting. Someone would pass. The grounds here and for miles around Blanco would be seen for many years. Long after his horse spirit should have left him. He roams the canyons and mesas. Never seen until the time for a passing. I heard about Tom Sullivan. I heard that he had seen the pale horse just before his passing. It is to be believed."

With that, Little Hawk went silent. We sipped our coffee in silence. After a while he arose from his chair and walked to the far side of the room, opened a drawer in a small cabinet. He returned to the table and placed a worn pair of silver spurs in front of me. "These are for you, Sergeant Bob. I have no more use for them," he said. I protested. He would have none of it. "You must understand. Just before your arrival I saw the pale horse. It is my time," he said. Again, I protested— to no good. Little Hawk then said, "You must leave now. I must prepare for my journey."

I stepped out the door. The wind was cold. I pulled my jacket around me, and left Little Hawk to his business.

Little Hawk was found on his bed the next day by a game warden who had stopped by to visit with him. He appeared to have passed peacefully.

Did I believe the story about the pale horse? Had I seen *Blanco* on that mesa that evening? Not all who saw the pony passed, just those whose time it was. Not my time yet? But, when I'm out in the canyons I admit to glancing up. Looking at the mesas. Looking for the pale horse. The fabled ... Death Horse.

MS. CARTER'S RED SAUCE

It was the first cold snap of the season. And as a ritual of sorts with me, I started my first pot of Texas Chili of the winter. I shuffled around my little apartment kitchen getting this and that for my chili. I got all the ingredients ready, dumped them in my old cast iron pot that was on the stove, and turned on the flame. The smell of homemade chili soon filled my apartment. I let it simmer. Watched some football. Back and forth from my old recliner to the kitchen to stir my chili pot. Then I got a spoon full and took a little taste. WTF? Something wasn't right! But, what? Ahh ... then I remembered. I had forgot to add some of Ms. Carter's homemade "red sauce" (And if you don't know what Chili Red Sauce is, we can't be friends.) I looked through my kitchen cabinet. No "red sauce"! %&*&^%! I would have to drive over to Ms. Crater's house and get some! Can't have Texas Chili without *red sauce*. And Ms. Carter's was the best!

I put on my big wool jacket, boots and old tattered Stetson and headed over to Ms. Carter's. North wind howling. Cloudy.

Cold. Ms. Carter lived on the south side. Little stone and wood house. The thing being that you just knocked on her door and she would open and you would just say you needed some "red sauce". She would turn and go back somewhere and bring back a bottle. Five bucks. She brought it to you and you paid and left. Ms. Carter was this wisp of a woman. A widow. Long gray hair in a bun. Long flour sack dress.

But this time when I knocked and she answered the door, she looked terrible. Eyes red. Skin clammy. Very pale. She saw it was me and swung the door open wide and said, "Sergeant! So glad to see you! Please, come in!" *Huh?* I had been to get chili sauce for years— never invited in her house. I walked in. Nice little living room. Clean as a pin. She looked at me with a deep frown. "Sergeant, there's something in my house. A shadow. It comes out at night. It scares me."

A shadow? Scaring Ms. Carter? WT? But I was there and she was clearly needing help ...

So, having told Ms. Carter I would help with the "shadows" she was seeing at night in her bedroom I left her house and drove back to my little apartment. I had left my pot of Texas Chili on a slow simmer on the stove. I turned the fire off, took my Glock .40 off my nightstand and shoved it into my belt. Wasn't expecting to need it, but in my business ... better safe than sorry. Ms. Carter had said she would go spend the night with her sister and gave me the key to her house.

About 10 o'clock that night I drove back over to Ms. Carter's. Cold. Wind blowing hard. I let myself in and wondered what kind of "shadows" were causing her such distress. I turned on the living room light and walked back to Ms. Carter's bedroom. Small, with a small bed. Nightstand. Dresser. I didn't turn on the lamp on the nightstand. Dark. Her bed had a beautiful rose quilt across it. Handmade, I would bet. Having nowhere to sit I eased on her bed and leaned back against the backboard— and waited. At some point I dozed off. I stirred a bit a little later and opened one eye— and saw it. The "shadow". On the far wall. Kinda blurry. But crawling across said wall. I opened my other eye. Tensed. No real "shape". WT? A "scratching" sound from somewhere. Okay, the hair on my arms stood up! I watched. No real threat, but very disturbing! I watched. The shadow seemed to move back and forth. The scratching continued. And then I glanced to the window behind the bed. And saw it. Mystery solved! *Whew*! There was a large mesquite bush outside the window. The wind was blowing and the streetlight on the corner threw the "shadow" of the bush against the wall! The scratching was the bush against the window! I got up and walked to the window and closed the curtain. No shadow!

The next morning, I called Ms. Crater at her sister's house. Explained the shadow. She was appreciative!

Moral of this story is that while something may not be "normal" it doesn't necessarily mean its "para" normal.

And I got TWO bottles of Ms. Carters Red Sauce for the price of one! My Chili was complete! With crackers and ketchup, it was delicious!

A win-win this time! But, little did I know that things were about to change ...

THE BANSHEE WAIL

It was late. Nearly dusk outside. I was just wrapping up my reports and looking forward to getting home. Dr. Jack and coke ... maybe a pizza and then an early bed. The phone on my desk rang. I looked at it, ignore it. Whatever it was could wait till tomorrow. But ... dammit! I answered. Father Henry. Could I come over to the church and meet him? &^%&*&! But, yeah. Okay. I would go see him.

The drive over to Saint Vincent's was a short drive, a few blocks up on the north end. Nice older church. Stone and wood. I parked my Tahoe out front and got out and started to the front door. Didn't get far. Father Henry came out in a hurry. Father Henry was portly, with a big stock of gray hair on his head. His frock tight around him. He stopped and looked at me and said, "I have to go to the Baxter's. Something has happened and I don't really want to go alone, so come along my son." He started walking toward my Tahoe, looked over his shoulder at me and said, "They have had a banshee visit!" WT? A *BANSHEE*? Everything I knew about banshees could fit on the head of a pin! And I didn't think I needed to know anything more! But I got in my Tahoe next to Father Henry and off we went. Banshees. What was I about to get into now ... ?

It was full dark when we got to the Baxter's house. Nice little frame home. Quite street. Just how a frickin' banshee ended up here in a small West Texas town I had no idea! Didn't really care! I didn't want any part of it! We got out of my Tahoe and walked to the front door. It swung open before we could even knock! Mr. Baxter stood just inside and said, "Come in ... come in." Older guy. Dressed in a pull over sweater and jeans. We walked in. Mr. Baxter was in a tizzy, it seemed. Mrs. Baxter stood in the living room and her eyes were red. She had been crying, it looked like. Short, stout little woman. Gray hair. Wearing a plain blue dress. I stood back. I had no idea what I was doing there other than Father Henry had asked me to come with him. Father Henry looked back over his shoulder at me and introduced me to the Baxters. They paid no attention to me. They were both talking at once to Father. I backed further away. Didn't want any part of whatever was going on with the Baxter's and banshees!

As they were yapping at full speed with the Father, I eased back out the door onto the porch. Had a seat in the porch swing and waited. Heard then going at it for another fifteen minutes. I waited. Then it got quiet.

Father came out the front door and looked at me. He said, "Mr. Baxter says he heard a banshee last night. The *wail*. But, didn't see her. If he hears *and* sees her then she is foreboding his death. He wants us to stay the night here with them. So, we will." It wasn't a request. It was a statement. Father walked back in the house.

And so, I sit in the swing. Just what Father expected me to do with a frickin' banshee I didn't know. But I sit and waited. The Baxters, Father, and I. Waiting on a banshee ...

It was a pleasant night. Not too hot. I took my gun belt off and laid it down on the porch. Laid back in the swing and drifted off. Don't know for how long before I heard it. A "shrill" sound. High pitched. I bolted upright! Trying to wake up and understand what I was hearing! Then a commotion in the house! Loud voices! I could hear Father's voice loudly! I jumped up off the swing, reached down and grabbed my Glock .40 out of its holster and ran to the door and opened it! And when I did a flash of red and green! I couldn't believe what my baby blues were seeing! The *shrill* was loud! It came toward me! I ducked as it got to me! An ice-cold blast as it went past me and out the closed door! WTF!

I turned to see Father standing in the middle of the living room. Drenched in sweat! His frock torn open. His head down. He was mumbling. He looked up to me and said, "I failed. She took Baxter." He turned and walked back toward the bedroom. She? She, *who?* WT was that about?

The ambulance was, of course, too late. Ms. Baxter crying. Father was distraught. The autopsy later said, massive coronary failure. Truth be told whatever I had seen damn near gave me a coronary!

I didn't tell anyone about that night. Ms. Baxter and Father knew. I mean what was I going to say? That I had heard and seen a *banshee*, In a small isolated West Texas town.

I'm still a little nervous when I hear certain high-pitched sounds. Not fond of red and green either. But banshees? Impossible ... right?

THIS TIME

I hung up the phone and leaned back in my old office chair. Thought about the call for a moment. Stood up, adjusted the Glock .40 on my hip, took my battered Stetson off my desk and walked out my office door.

LEOs work all the cases as best they can. But, this time ... this time it was personal.

It had been a cold February. Exactly one year ago today. The call all officers hate! Tragic! A child had died. And the worst part— murdered. Details here are not relevant. Won't go there. Suffice to say it was bad. Her name was Samantha. Twelve years old. Found late one evening behind the school. She hadn't got off the school bus and her mother, Renee, had called. Frantic. The school bus driver had been contacted and said Sam hadn't got on the bus. She called the Sheriff's Department. We started a search. But it was a teacher walking to her car in the school parking lot that had saw "something" on the edge of the field behind the school. It had been Sam. Pretty little girl. Red hair.

From there the situation goes like any would in this type of matter. Renee was contacted. Hysterical. And then the investigation began. Long hours. Multiple agencies assisting. Not much evidence. Many months. Talking to everybody. Interviewing people. Being somewhat isolated in our small little West Texas town strangers would be seen. Some locals said a man with a "straw" hat had been seen around town. Nothing would come of that. Still all law enforcement officers worked! Not giving up! Her murderer would be found and they would pay! But, the days, weeks, and months passed. Nothing.

So, when Renee had called me to tell me "Sam" had been there at home last night I didn't question her. Just got in my old patrol car and went to Renee's little south side home. In a residential neighborhood. Neat yard and house. Renee was a widow. Her husband had been killed in a car wreck years ago and she was a secretary at a local insurance office. Sam had been an only child.

I parked on the street out front and walked to the door and knocked. Renee opened the door immediately and said, "She was here! In her room! I saw her!".

I walked into the house to listen to a mother who told me a story about having seen her dead daughter ...

Small living room. Clean. Couch, coffee table, two chairs. Large screen TV. Renee was wearing jeans, blouse and barefoot. Her red hair tied back in a ponytail. And very nervous. She repeated that she had seen Sam. Sam had been in her bedroom at the back of the house. I didn't know how to respond to her. Obviously, she hadn't actually *seen* Sam. But she seemed so upset that I asked her to show me where she had saw her. She led me back to Sam's bedroom and opened the door. Nothing had changed since the last time I had been there. During the "investigation" we had routinely searched Sam's room looking for any clues that might help find her killer. Didn't find anything. Sam's room was a typical girl's room with this and that on the walls, a small writing desk and some dolls on the bed.

"She was sitting at her desk. She turned and looked at me when I walked by," Renee said.

I just looked around the room.

"Would you like some coffee?" Renee asked.

I said yes and Renee walked back toward the kitchen. It was dusk now and Renee had turned the light on when we walked into Sam's room. Nothing more to see here. An empty bedroom. I turned to walk out and switched the light off. And just as I did ... I heard a voice behind me. More of a whisper. I turned around to see a *shadow* at the writing desk. Small, but clearly a little girl. Not quite visible but there. I just stood looking at the "girl's shadow". She appeared to be looking directly at me. And then she said, "Sir ..." Nothing more. Just "Sir". I stepped back, taken off guard at what I was seeing. And then she was gone. Just ... gone.

I stood at the door, looking in the empty room. What did that *shadow* say? *Sir?* What could that mean? No idea. But I was damned sure going to find out ...

I stepped back into the hall. Not knowing what to think. What had I seen? What had I heard? A *ghost?* I walked back into the living room, where Renee had my cup of coffee waiting for me. I needed it. I didn't tell her what I had seen. What was I going to say? That I had seen her dead daughter? We talked a few minutes. I told her I believed she had seen something. Wasn't going to acknowledge I had seen "Sam" the same as she had.

I left promising Renee that I was not going to rest till Sam's killer was caught. So much time had passed. A year. But, none of us at the Sheriff's Department were slacking off. No matter how long it took. Her killer was still out there.

Whatever I had seen had said one word ... *Sir.* If I was to believe what I had heard was Sam's ghost what did she mean? "Sir" could be any "man". But, the last place "Sam" had been seen was the school. Her body had been found next to the school. So back to the school I would go.

We had interviewed every teacher, janitor, student, and employee at the school but Sam's ghost was telling me *sir.*

And if she was trying to tell me something about *sir* ... I was damned well going to find him ...

TWO–PASS MOUNTAIN

Some may remember that I mentioned that I like Texas history. I have visited most of the old Texas forts ...

I had heard stories of an old "stage stop" up on Two-Pass Mountain. So called, obviously, because there were two "passes" through the mountain. So, when I was able to get a few days off I headed west to go see if I could find that old stage stop. About 40 miles to the turn off from paved blacktop to a barely discernible dirt road. I had been told how to get where I was headed from some old timers around town, who claimed that they had been told about it years ago. But none had actually been there. Just been told about it.

It was a cold March day, and I was prepared. Heavy coat and boots. I had packed for an overnight trip. Tent and supplies. A few sandwiches, canteen of water. All in a backpack I was going to trek in with, since there was no road to where I was going. The property the old place was supposed to be on belonged to the Henderson family and the only Henderson I could find was a lady in San Angelo. She had said she had heard about the old stage stop from her grandfather but hadn't been out there. Just desolate rocks and canyons. She gave me permission to go looking and wished me luck. She said her Grandfather had told her that he himself had just kind of stumbled on it while hunting. Told her he would never go back anywhere around it. Said he seemed afraid of the place, for whatever reason, but never told her why.

The day had turned cloudy and overcast as I reached the end of the road. Just dead ended into a small canyon. I parked, got my backpack on and started walking. An ominous feeling nagging at me as I hiked ...

The west Texas sky was getting darker as I trudged along. The backpack heavy. Night doesn't fall on you in west Texas, it eases in and lays on you like blanket. Since there was no trail up to the mountain I was looking for "land marks" that the old timers had given me. The canyon forked about two miles in and I veered to the left. The north wind had increased and I decided I needed to stop and make camp before night enveloped me.

On a semi-level ledge, I took off the backpack and started setting up. The tent, bed roll ... camp stuff. I got some rocks together in a circle and found branches of mesquite and started a fire. Desolate out there. Just me and mother nature. The quite was actually a little disconcerting. I heated up some stew over the fire. Cold biscuits. As I ate, I reflected on what I heard about the old stage stop. Built as a stop for the stage between Fort Davis and San Angelo. But, for some reason it had been abandoned after only a couple of months. Something about "spirits" heard at night. Visions of things on full moons. The pioneers were a superstitious lot and the operators of the stage stop had packed up and left in a hurry. And the stage stop was left alone and forgotten about up on the mountain.

It was late and my fire was going out. And cold. I unrolled my bed in the tent and lay down. I still had a long way to go. My "duty weapon", a GLOCK .40, beside me. Wasn't thinking about needing it but the nights in west Texas can have feelings. I dozed off. Wondering about the legends of that old stage stop. Got a chill. What was coming ... ?

The day dawned cloudy and cold. I rolled out of my sleeping bag, stood up and stretched. Hadn't slept well. Had dreams. Or nightmares. Didn't know which but it didn't bode well for me. I reached in my backpack and got two pieces of jerky. Breakfast. Pulled on my boots, straightened my jeans, stuffed my Glock .40 in my jeans and broke camp.

The sun was trying to break through the clouds over Two-Pass Mountain in the distance. I heaved the backpack over my shoulders and started walking.

Keeping to the left of the forked canyon. Rough terrain. Boulders, rocks, mesquite. But I was focused on finding that old stage stop. My love of Texas history overshadowing the legends of spirits and such.

Three hours of hiking brought me to the base of the mountain. The two passes that the mountain was named for could be seen from where I was standing. One to the left. One to the right. Here I veered to the right as I was told that a small trail would head up the face of the mountain. I found the old trail and started climbing. Stopping to rest every 30 minutes or so to catch my breath. Up the trail led. I hiked on. Switchbacks and turns. And on I hiked. At a large boulder against a dry spring, I cut sharp to the left. As I came around the boulder ... I saw it. Some broken stone walls. The remains of a mesquite wood corral. I was relived and excited.

I hiked up closer the old stage stop picturing in my mind the stages stopping, the horses being tended to. The stories those falling down stone walls could tell!

The sun was falling and the night was creeping. I found a small cliff overhang about fifty yards to the north of the stage stop. I took my backpack off and started setting up camp, then made a small fire. The wind that had died down was starting to pick up again. Cloudy and getting colder with night falling. I wanted to make my way down to the old stage stop and start exploring. But night was falling fast. My exploring would have to wait till tomorrow. I settled in my tent with more jerky for my supper. I was tired. I lay back on my bed roll, needing sleep.

But, little did I know that there would be no sleep for me that night. The cold wind hinting at a night that would be what nightmares are made of ...

I lay on my bed roll trying to sleep, dozing of ... when I heard it. A low ... *howl*. The wind. Nothing more. But, nothing like I ever heard before. I tossed and turned. The howl incessant. I raised up to listen. I rolled out of my bedroll and came to my knees. Dark. I pulled the tent flap back and stepped out. The full moon in and out of the clouds. I heard *hoof beats*. Horses? *Nah*. But I swore I could hear the neighing of horses! Impossible! Nothing out here but me up on this mountain!

The howl grew louder. I stood outside my tent perplexed! The howl ... the horses. The full moon broke between the clouds and I saw it. Three riders on horses! The full moon showing clearly ... Indians! Just above the old stage stop! Riding in circles! I stood, frozen. Watching the specters! Their appearance gray and transparent! Their horses as black as the night! The howling louder! I stumbled backwards! My mind telling me what I was seeing was impossible but my eyes telling me it was true! I was watching what had made the stage stop crew abandon the place! The "spirit" legend. Right in front of me! Around and around the stage stop they rode! The howl now so loud I had to cover my ears! I was confused and I admit— scared! The impossible was happening in front of me! Then the specters seemed to see me standing there. Their horses reared and they galloped toward me! I panicked! I fell to the ground and covered my head as I heard them gallop over me! I rolled over to see where they were at! I didn't see them! Gone! But, how? They were right on top of me! I jumped up and stumbled back in my tent. Jerked my boots on and grabbed my Glock .40, having no idea what I was going to do with my gun! Shoot them? I stood in my tent shaking! I couldn't stay there all night. I wasn't being rational! I was confused and not thinking about anything but the first law of nature ... self-preservation! I had to do something! So, I took a deep breath and stepped out of the tent. The howling had subsided. Nothing out here now. But I know what I saw! What I heard! I stood looking around. Nothing. I turned and went back in my tent and sat on my bed roll. Listening. For how long I don't know. Hours? And then I could see a little light outside. Daybreak! I stepped out and could see the sun coming up! I started grabbing my stuff. Stuffed it all in my backpack, zipped up my wool jacket and started off back down the mountain. Forgetting about exploring the old stage stop. I found myself half running, half jogging down that mountain. Hours. Night approaching. I didn't stop. Down the mountain I went. The bottom and jogged to my truck! And I backed out on the trail road and drove away. Fast!

Time passed. I never told anyone about that night up on Two-Pass Mountain. Why would I? Nobody would believe me. Just legends about that place.

If you have followed my stories you know that as a cop I have encountered some strange and unexplained issues. None really scared me. But, Two-Pass mountain had scared this cop. For the first time something *paranormal* had really scared me. I moved on with my life. But, had nightmares now and then. Heard a howl, saw specters. Just nightmares. That's all. Just nightmares ...

INCIDENT AT RIKER'S CAVE

I had heard about it. From fellow *rock kickers*. Riker's Cave. And I was curious. I hunt Indian arrowheads. Had a nice collection. None of my buds had actually been there but they figured it would be a good place to maybe find some nice *points*. I knew where the old Riker ranch was. Nothing much left out there— just an old tumbled down ranch house. A few rotting corrals. The place had been abandoned years ago by the family. It was about 25 miles out in the far west end of the county. In a dead-end canyon. Off the main two-lane blacktop about 10 miles. Nothing but dust, canyons, and mesquite out there. But I thought about what I had been told about Riker's Cave and commenced to trying to locate the land owner. Didn't go poking around on private property out here. That could get you shot. I went to the County Tax Office and was able to go through the records and find that a lady named Barb Riker owned the land and place out there. She lived in San Antonio. I found a phone number and gave her a call. She answered the phone, and I explained who I was and asked if I could have permission to go out and kick some rock and look for points. She was amiable. Then I asked her about the "cave". She hesitated. She said it may not be a good idea to go poking around that cave. I asked why and she just said "bad juju". I didn't believe in "juju" bad or otherwise. She said okay and related she had only been out to the cave once as a little girl with her dad. Her dad had taken her out with him looking for "strays". He had pointed the "cave" out to her but didn't take her around it. She gave me general directions and said it I would have to hike in. Before she hung up the phone she said, "You might ought to let somebody know you're going to be out there. In case you don't come back they will know where to come looking for you." And she hung up.

So, the next morning I called dispatch, told them about where I would be that day, filled my backpack with my canteen, gloves, my short shovel for digging and my sawed off .410 Shotgun. Rattlesnakes were always a risk poking around in that country.

I loaded up my old Jeep and headed west. Pretty fall day. Hoped to find some good points around that old cave. But, couldn't help but wonder. Bad "juju"? What did she mean by that ... ?

My old Jeep Wrangler, though rough looking with dings and scrapes and dents, purred along the two-lane blacktop. The miles flying past. About 40 miles along I finally saw the double boulders she had told me about. "Turn right there", she had said. Thing is, out here you didn't give directions in miles or such. You gave landmarks to determine where you were or where you were going. Turn right at the two boulders, go about two miles in and you will see the rotting fence posts. Follow the posts for about another 3 or four miles and you will see a clump of mesquites. "That's as far as you can drive in", she had said. From there it was a far piece along the canyon wall till the canyon forked. "Take the left fork and look up," she had said. I parked my Jeep and looked around. Miles and miles of nothing but rocks and mesquites.

I walked around the back of my Jeep, grabbed my backpack, threw it over my shoulder and started hiking. Nice day. My old tattered Stetson keeping the West Texas sun off my head. I hiked. Finally saw the canyon rim. I angled to the left and continued. Stopping here and there for a rest. Drinking a little water from my canteen. I shifted my backpack and kept hiking. The canyon did fork and I angled left. Rough hiking. No trail. Just around and over boulders, rocks and scrub brush. Always looking down. Rattlesnake country. The sun was high when I glanced up and saw it. The mouth of the cave. Odd. A chill came over me. I started climbing. Up and over boulders, rocks and mesquite. Then a little "ledge". I managed to stand on it and could see the mouth of the Cave clearly now. 'Bout fifteen foot across ... ten feet to the top. I stood looking around. Reached over my shoulder and got my little digging shovel from my backpack. As I walked toward the mouth of the cave I was looking down and around. Arrowheads. Hoped to find some. Saw some worked flint scattered around. Good sign! Working my way toward the mouth of the Cave. Another chill. A little strange but nothing to be concerned about. But, a few feet from the cave. I heard it. Kinda like an echo. But no mistaking what the sound was. A low, distinct "growl". Not an animal growl. Not a human growl. And I didn't like the sound of it ...

And so, it was at that point that I stopped looking down for points and started looking at the mouth of the cave. It had been a growl, of sorts. I had heard coyote growls, mountain lion growls, and even bear growls. The cave growl had been nothing like those. It was as if the cave itself had growled. I eased closer to the mouth of the cave. Stepping around small boulders and being careful not to step to close to the ledge— and I stood at the mouth and looked in. Couldn't see how far back it went. I stepped in a few feet. Just as far as I could see. Then stopped. Dark any further in. Nope. Not going any further. Spelunker I wasn't. No sound now. I backed out into the sun. Still looking in the mouth. No idea what to make of the growl. Fairly certain it wasn't an animal. And then the growl again, low ... and a hiss. I Stepped further back. Nope. Again. Whatever that was, I didn't want to aggravate it. "See something?" A voice behind me said.

Startled I jumped and turned around to see a young guy a few yards down the ledge looking up at me. WT? Where did he come from? He was dressed in a blue flannel shirt, jeans, dusty cowboy boots and a sweat stained straw hat. He was grinning at me. "*Uhh*, no ... didn't see anything. Just heard something," I said to him. He continued grinning and said, "Yeah. The cave was talking to you. Warning you. Bet you heard a growl, didn't you?" I said, "Well, something like that." He motioned me down to him saying, "I'm Jason Riker. Come down a ways. There's shade under the ledge and I will tell you something about that cave. And why I won't get any closer to it."

Still a little taken aback by him just being behind me like he had been, I eased back down the ledge toward him.

He turned and walked back down the ledge a ways and stopped. There was an overhang and he sat on a boulder, in the shade. I followed and sat down beside him. He was still grinning. "You looking for the silver?" He asked. *Silver?* "Silver?" I asked. "Yeah", he answered. "*Uhh* ... no, I'm looking for points," I said. "Oh," he said and continued. "Maybe some around but I never saw any. Figured you were looking for the silver that's supposed to be in that cave. I shook my head, "Nope, don't know anything about any silver."

"Well, legend says the Padres from Mission San Saba mined silver out of that cave. Back sometime in the 1700's. The Padres even camped here for a while. Mining that silver. Legend says that a cowboy even found bones at the entrance wearing brown wraps like the Padres used to wear. An Indian arrow stuck in his back. And some people have found their way out here to look for silver in the cave. But none would go in. Say that the cave *growled* when they started to go in and they took tail and left! Some say the cave wouldn't let nobody but the Padres work in it, and when the Indians killed them the cave warned people to stay out with a growl or a hiss," he said. I sat looking at young guy and frowned. "Well, I did hear something that sounded like a growl or hiss when I stood at the entrance", I admitted.

"I used to come out here with dad once in a while looking for strays, and he would point up here to the cave and tell me to never come around it", he said. "Guess you talked to my sister about coming out here," he continued.

"Well, didn't know she was your sister but if you're a Riker I guess I did," I replied.

"Yeah. My sister. I'm Jason," he said.

We sat a few minutes not talking. I asked, "You never went in the cave yourself looking for that silver?"

He didn't say anything for a while. He mumbled, "Yeah. I did. Didn't work out well." Then he said, "I got to go now." And just stood up and waked back down the ledge leaving me sitting there.

WT? Then I thought— *where did he come from?* He didn't have a backpack or anything. Long hike into this place from anywhere. He had just been there behind me. He was out of sight now. No idea where he went. It was getting late and I hadn't found any points so I started the long hike back to my Jeep. I stopped and looked back over my shoulder at the cave. Could swear I heard a hiss. I hiked back to my Jeep and left.

The next day I called Ms. Riker to thank her for giving me permission to go out there and mentioned I had seen her brother Jason. Silence on her end. Then she said, "Sergeant, I have no idea who you saw and talked to, but it wasn't my brother Jason. He was found dead just inside that cave ten years ago ..."

CASSIE

I had seen her off and on for over a year, I guess. Always at night. Out on Spring Canyon Road. Far north end of the County. Nothing much out that way. A few isolated ranches. Two lane blacktop that wound around the canyon for about five miles. She was never in the same place. Over here. Over there. Off the road maybe fifty yards or so. I say "seen her". But of course, that wasn't possible. She wasn't really "there". Just a specter ... a vague vision. Could make out a dress, long hair on a lady's head. Not her face. I had stopped a couple of times to just stare. She seemed to look in my direction ... and disappear. Just gone. I never mentioned her to anyone. What would I say? I had seen a ghost? Nope.

But, after seeing her one day after making my rounds I decided to maybe ask somebody. But who? Only one I could think of would be Jess. Didn't even know his last name. Just Jess. Had a small place about two miles off the road at a bend in the canyon. Had been there forever, it seemed. As long as I had been there. Didn't look forward to talking to him though.

A disagreeable sort. A hermit, people said. Just didn't like people in general. But he had been out here in the canyons for years. He might know something. So that night I turned by the old corral and drove toward Jess' place. He might talk to me. Might not. But I was curious about "her"... so I drove my old patrol car down that dusty road, wondering what he might he ... ?

But about halfway down the dirt road to Jess' place I got a call. A burglary in town. I turned around and headed back to town. Kinda forgot about that vision. The specter of the lady. It was about a week later on a hot summer day that I remembered. I drove my old patrol car out of town. Toward Jess place.

The dust flew up behind my patrol car as I drove— the AC straining to cool. I didn't make it all the way to Jess'. Saw him about a mile from his place. On the side of the dirt road, twisting some barbwire between fence posts. I stopped. Didn't pull off to the side of the road. Nobody likely to be coming down here to Jess' place. Jess was wearing a faded pair of blue jeans, a dirty red shirt, and old cowboy boots that had seen better days. A straw hat on his head that was sweat stained. His gray beard long. Creases on his face from long hot summer days. He squinted his eyes looking at me as I got out of my car. I walked up to him, nodded my head and said, "Jess". Didn't offer to shake hands. He wouldn't have shaken anyway. He didn't return my greeting. Just stood with the pliers in his hand looking at me. Jess was not a sociable type. I said, "Jess. I'm kinda curious about something. Thought you might be able to help."

He just looked at me. I waited. He finally said, "What is this about, Sergeant?"

I took a deep breath and told him about seeing the specter of the woman on Canyon drive at night. I finished talking. And waited. Jess might just think I was crazy. He just stood looking at me, then he said, "I don't know what you're talking about and I got work to do."

He turned away from me and started twisting the barb wire again. Okay. It had been worth a try. I turned and started walking back to my car. After a few steps he called after me, "And that lady you're talking about has a name! It's Cassie! And I might know a little something 'bout her. And I'm all out of tobacco."

The implication was clear. Some tobacco might entice him to talk some about *Cassie*. I just looked at him and nodded my head and continued walking. "But you're not likely to believe me when I tell you anyway," he muttered. "She's been dead over a hundred years."

He bent over the fence and started working again. I got in my patrol car, turned it around and headed out back toward town. I had to buy some chewing tobacco.

I drove into town and stopped at Buster's Drive-Inn. Got two bags of "chaw" and two bottles of cold water and drove back out to Jess' place. Texas' August sun blistering. I found Jess where I had left him, twisting barb wire between the fence post. I stopped. He looked over at me, straightened up and walked to my car, opened the passenger side door and got in. The AC in my old patrol car straining against the oppressive heat.

"Got my chaw?" He asked. His skin glistening with sweat. I handed him the two bags.

He took off the old, sweat stained straw hat, opened one bag took a big bite of "chaw" and leaned back in the seat. I reached over in the back seat, got the two bottles of water that weren't cold any longer, and gave him one. We opened the water. And he began ...

"Ain't no use telling you about Cassie. Just a legend more than anything. But a deal is a deal."

"It was right after the civil war. My great-great-grand daddy and his family and several others came here from New Orleans with the Overseer. Blanton was his name and since there was nothing much left in New Orleans, Blanton decided to try his hand at ranching and came here with all the others and bought a hundred acres and started ranching. Hard life it was. But a few small houses and corrals were built and most everybody that had come with Blanton stayed on working for him. The men folk working the ranch, the women folk taking care of the main house, cooking, cleaning and such. But Blanton was a hard, nasty soul. Treated everybody bad. Cassie was 'bout 15-year-old. Like the other women folk she worked around the house doing this and that. Blanton took a shine to her. Pretty girl that she was. He started abusing her. Doing stuff to her. She was scared to tell her maw and paw about it. It went on for a good spell. Then of a sudden she got with child. Her maw and paw were terrible upset of course. She wouldn't tell them who the daddy was. Until one day she just couldn't take the shame no more. She kinda blurted out to her maw 'bout Blanton being the daddy. She then ran outta the house. Long story short they didn't find her till 'bout a week later. Out on one of the trails, on the far side of the canyon. Dead. Died of thirst or such it appeared. They brought her back to the ranch and buried her out back. Nothing was done with Blanton. Men folk were scared of him. They had put a small wooden cross with her name Cassie on it over her grave. But, wasn't long they saw the grave had been disturbed. Cassie wasn't in it anymore. It was figured that Blanton couldn't stand seeing that grave and had moved her somewheres. And that was the end of it. Nothing more was said about Cassie. It was sometime later that folks started whispering about a *ghost* of sorts here 'bouts. Could see that it was girl, in the distance. Kinda *shimmering* in the moonlight. That's the story that was passed down in my family for generations. Cassie was still around. My folks bought this piece of land I'm living on, way back then. And I don't really give a damn if you believe me or not. I've seen her! Here and there, at night wandering around these canyons. Looking for her rightful grave I expect. But, she sure as hell is still around!"

With that Jess took a long drink of water. Put his old straw hat back on, said, "'Preciate the chaw." And got out. He walked back over to the fence and went back to work. I left.

Did I believe Jess? *Ghost* of a long dead girl wandering these canyons and roads looking for her rightful grave? Can't really say. But I know what I saw on some of those long, lonely nights driving through these parts. I saw "something". It did look like a girl in the distance.

But I never told anyone what Jess had told me. Who would believe the ramblings of an old, black hermit ...?

THREE SOULS DOWN

The wreckage of the small Piper Cub airplane sat about fifty yards past the runway. Burned. I was at the far airport gate waiting for the NTSB Investigators to arrive. It was a small airport. Mostly used by hunters that would fly into hunt for deer on the ranches thereabouts and by oil executives that would fly in to check the oil reserves and such. The plane had crashed the day before on takeoff. Three guys had been on board. Hunters that were flying back home to Houston. The plane had just attained liftoff when it stalled, went nose down and cartwheeled, caught fire when it hit the ground.

The fire department had responded and put the fire out. The wreckage had been confined to a small area. Nothing could be done for the victims that were surely in the wreckage. The closest NTSB office was in Austin. They had been called and I went out to meet them the next day. I would do a short information report and relate that the NTSB would do the investigation. Airplane crashes were not in my job description. The fire department had a couple of guys stand-by all night in case of a re-fire. It didn't. Newt Brown, the airport Supervisor, had taken the flight plan from the pilot before the take-off. Had seen the pilot and the two hunters board the plane on the runway, take off and crash, exploded on impact. No chance anyone could have survived that.

I was prepared to give the NTSB investigators a briefing and leave.

They arrived. Two guys, in a large SUV. I briefed them and just backed off and watched them get some stuff out of the SUV and start their job. I sat in my Tahoe and watched. After about an hour, one of them walked over to me.

He looked at me and said, "Who removed the three souls' remains?" *Huh*? Nobody had done anything like that. He stared at me and said, "Well, there are no remains of the three souls in that wreckage."

Three souls. Not where they should be ...

Notice: Be advised that parts of this story are graphic. Some readers may find this to be disconcerting. If graphic content offends you, please scroll past.

I had no idea how to respond to the NTSB Investigators. No bodies? No body parts? Crashed airplanes weren't in my job description. Obviously, the bodies or parts thereof had to be around somewhere. Three guys on board when it crashed. That was a fact. All three had been seen boarding.

They asked if I could call for some volunteers to come and search a larger area around the crash site. I called Dispatch who in turn called the Fire Department and presently several guys showed up. We started a grid search. Hundred yard grids. Walking. Searching. One, two hours. Then three. Nothing. It was getting dark. We suspended our search, and I was tired. Went home, had two shots of Dr. Jack and crashed.

The next morning after biscuits and gravy at Kathy's, I arrived at my office. Took off my old battered Stetson, laid it on my desk, shifted my Glock .40 on my waist and settled in my old desk chair. I knew that the NTSB investigators and the FD volunteers were going back this morning to continue the search for the bodies. But I had other cases that needed my attention and wasn't going back to the airport to help. Part of my morning routine was going through the night shift reports. About halfway through I saw a report from one of the deputies. He had responded to a call of "noises" around the airport hangar. He had went and reported he didn't hear any noises but did see "something" down around the plane crash sight. Didn't know exactly what it was. Just a "shimmering". Probably just plane parts in the moonlight he concluded. But the shimmering had moved as he watched. *Humph.*

If the bodies weren't recovered today, I might go and poke around the Airport tonight ...

I hadn't heard from any of the volunteers at the airport about finding the bodies or body parts. They had been told to call if they found anything. No call. So, nothing found. I finished the last of my reports and it was getting late. I leaned back in my old desk chair, sighed and stood up. I picked up my tattered Stetson from the desk, shifted the Glock .40 on my waist and left my office. Drove to my little apartment and took off my gun belt, popped the top of a cold beer and put a pizza in the oven. Sat down in my old recliner, leaned back and reflected. Three souls down in that crash. No bodies found. Anywhere. But common sense said the bodies had to be there. Somewhere. A deputy had seen "something". Shimmering in the distance at the crash site, he said. Humph. Well, I didn't have any answers. Yet. The pizza was ready. I ate a few bites. Wasn't really hungry. I changed into an old pair of jeans, a worn sports shirt and old Tony Llama boots, put my Glock. 40 under my belt and left for the airport.

The airport was a couple of miles north of town. The gate wasn't locked. I got out of my Tahoe, opened the gate and drove in. Dark. Two lights— one on a pole at the little airport manager's office and the other hanging over the hanger doors at the back end of the field. I drove up in front of the office and parked. The runway long and dark. I turned the motor off, window down. And waited. Not knowing exactly what I was looking to see. I was staring at the far end of the runway where the plane had gone down. Really dark down that way. And the air ... it seemed *heavy*. All around.

And then I saw them. I eased out of my Tahoe. I leaned against the door, lit a cigarette and watched. Three "shimmering" lights at the far end of the runway. They seemed to move about. I watched. Then took a last drag from my smoke. Not wanting to drive on the runway I started walking— a long walk— down toward the shimmering lights.

Down that runway to the end where the plane crashed. Dark. The three shimmering entities were still there, moving around. The closer I got the air seemed to get heavier. A low *hum* was around me. I kept walking. Then about fifty yards from the site the shimmering just disappeared. Gone. I stopped. Staring. The *hum* was gone also. Nothing except the heavy air.

I then continued walking. And the closer I got I could smell something. A smell I was all too familiar with. I knew that smell. Decomposing human flesh. I had investigated many cases that had that smell. No describing it. No mistaking it. I found myself at the crash site. Nothing there. It had all been cleaned up. Just a large burned area on the ground. So where was that smell coming from. The whole area had been searched. No bodies. No body parts.

I walked around awhile. In the dark. Nothing. I walked the long walk back down the runway to my Tahoe. I glanced back at the site. Nothing "shimmering" there now. But I know what I seen. My eyes didn't lie. I climbed back in my Tahoe and went home.

Cops want answers. Don't like opened ended mysteries. But answers never came. From time-to-time pilots and assorted workers reported "shimmering" entities at the end of that runway at night. NTSB had to come up with something for the families of the three that were in the plane. They finally just said that the bodies just burned on impact and nothing was retrievable. BS. I didn't buy that then, don't buy it now. Bones and torn body parts scattered around away from a crash site just don't get burned to dust.

And so, no answers. But I know what I had seen that dark night. Three "shimmering" entities. Three souls down.

And so, 'til next time ...

ACKNOWLEDGEMENTS

Publication was a big deal for dad, and I've been glad that he was excited about it. He wanted to thank the following ...

Doug Klein, without whom this book could not have been written. He had the "insight" to save my stories as I posted them on social media. I, personally, never saved any. He then created a backmatter blurb for the anthology. Many thanks.

The "Readers" of my stories. Each and every one encouraged me to publish a book. They were persistent, and I owed them the attempt at satisfying their requests. Thank you all of you!

And last but not least, to my son Ron. An accomplished author himself who acted as my publisher and guided my way through the process. Thank you, son. (*It was the least I could do, dad.*)

ABOUT THE AUTHOR

Robert Dean is a forty-year law enforcement veteran and Texas Master Peace Officer having served in agencies across Texas. He attained the rank of Lieutenant and Chief in two departments. He has a Bachelors Degree in Criminal Justice and over two thousand hours of LE training.

He served on the Alamo Area/Narcotics Task Force in San Antonio, Texas doing Intervention and Enforcement issues with violent South Texas gangs, and on the Attorney Generals Violent Gang Task Force, was Vice-President on the Board of Directors of the Texas ISD Police Chiefs Association as well as serving on the Board of Directors of the Texas Police Chiefs Association.

Having observed that some "cases" bordered on "paranormal" premises he wanted to document such cases giving rise to this book.

He is now retired and lives with his wife in Castroville, Texas.

www.ingramcontent.com/pod-product-compliance
Lightning Source LLC
Chambersburg PA
CBHW012019110726
47994CB00009B/3223